Revival

Shelter Book 3

ROBIN MERRILL

New Creation Publishing

New Creation Publishing
Madison, Maine

Chapter 1

Galen

When Galen heard the scream, he didn't even pick up his pace.

Wails of anger, frustration, and occasionally actual fear were commonplace at Open Door Church's homeless shelter. Years ago, each scream had scared him half to death, but now? Not so much.

As he grew closer, he heard a child crying—still a common sound, but one he wasn't desensitized to yet—and his worn-out boots did start to move faster.

The sounds grew clearer: a woman whimpering; a deep voice cursing; the child still crying. Galen rounded the last corner and a sharp pain stabbed at his chest. Hardly aware of it, he rubbed the spot with one hand. Chest pains were not a new thing. He chalked it up as just another symptom of getting older.

The doorway stood open and Galen stepped inside to find a short thin man pointing a handgun at a woman cowering on her knees in front of him. She looked at the floor, her hair hanging over her face, and it took Galen a second to recognize her. He stepped between the gun and the child to his right and held both hands out toward the man. "Damien, what's going on here?" He wondered whether he should look him in the eye. One should try to appear strong and confident when facing a grizzly. One should never look an aggressive dog in the eye. Eye contact showed someone you care. All these tidbits of advice raced through his mind and he finally decided he really had no choice. He had to look the man in the eye.

Damien returned his gaze. Despite the bright sunlight pouring through the window, his pupils were giant black saucers.

Galen swallowed, his mouth as dry as sand.

"I did a bad thing, Pastor." The words flew out quickly. "I ... I ... I ..." He wanted to say something more, but he couldn't.

"Well, Damien"—Galen took a small step forward, and Damien sidestepped to avoid Galen's advance, bumping his shoulder on the top bunk to his left—"you're certainly doing a bad thing right now. But you can stop this one."

Damien's eyes darted to the woman in front of him, then back to Galen, then back the woman again. "I know." He seemed resigned to Galen's suggestion, but he didn't lower his weapon.

"Why don't you give me the gun, Damien?" Galen turned one of his hands over, palm up. "We'll let Traci and Justin go, and then we'll make a plan. I'll help you, Damien."

He barely let Galen finish his offer. "No."

Galen took a long breath. "Why not? Help me understand."

He didn't say anything, and the wobbling of his outstretched arm grew worse.

Galen feared he was going to accidentally pull the trigger.

He made a noise: part groan, part whimper.

Galen dropped his arms. He no longer had the strength to keep them in the air. "Why are you pointing a gun at Traci?" He tried to hide his growing impatience. "Whatever she did, it doesn't deserve this."

Slowly, in a mouselike voice, Traci said, "I didn't do anything. He came in through the window—"

"Shut up!"

"Mommy," Justin whimpered.

Galen knew he wasn't deescalating the situation. He considered his options. Diplomacy wasn't working. There was a time when getting physical would've been his first choice, but he wasn't as young or as quick as he used to be—not that he was ever all that quick. He'd been a linebacker, not a running back. He could tackle Damien, easily take him down, but would the gun go off in the process? Probably. And if it did, what were the chances the stray bullet would hit Traci? Pretty good, he feared.

"Does this have anything to do with Traci? Or did she just happen to be here when you came through the window?" He wished he were better at negotiating.

Damien made another crying sound.

"I don't even know this guy," Traci said.

"I was trying to hide."

Good. That was something. "Okay, you can still hide. Just let them go."

Damien looked at him and snorted. "You're going to let me hide here?"

"Yes. At least until you explain to me what's going on."

A look of sheer terror fell over Damien's face like a curtain. "I think he might be dead."

Galen's stomach rolled. Who might be dead? Had Damien killed someone? Galen was used to operating in arenas he wasn't quite qualified for, but this might be too much. He swallowed again. "Who, Damien? Who might be dead?"

"The cop."

A hot wave of nausea washed over Galen, and he held one hand out to steady himself, though there was nothing nearby to grab. Damien had killed a cop? There was a cop killer standing in his church? No, he told himself, he didn't know that yet. He needed more information. "Why do you think he might be dead?"

Damien looked down at the floor and as he did so, the gun dropped a few inches. He went to wipe his nose with the back of his free hand, and Galen saw his opportunity. He lunged.

Chapter 2

Daniel

Daniel sat on the steel grating of his apartment's fire escape, his legs dangling over the edge. If he leaned ten inches to the left, he could see the waters of Portland Harbor, but that wasn't the view he cared about. He was looking down into the alley—at Ember.

She was his classmate, his neighbor, and his friend. But that was all. Though she told him he was the nicest guy she'd ever met, she had no interest in being his girlfriend, a fact that made him heartsick and kept him awake nights. He didn't know the man she was currently sharing a cigarette with, but he knew he was old. Much older than Daniel, and much too old for Ember. He was out of school, at least, maybe by a lot.

Ember's giggle drifted up to Daniel's perch and he grimaced. It wasn't real. He knew what her real laugh sounded like. He made her laugh all the time.

She leaned in and smashed her pink lips into the man's face, and Daniel had to look away. Did Ember know that he was up there watching her? He suspected that maybe she did. Sometimes he thought Ember enjoyed his affection, enjoyed getting it without giving anything in return. Part of him wished that one or both of them *would* see him sitting up there, see him drinking a beer at two in the afternoon. It would make him seem older.

He couldn't handle the kissing anymore. He pulled his legs up and pushed himself to a stand. He gave them one more glance—still lip-locked—and then he bent to climb back into the apartment he shared with his mother and her snake of a boyfriend. Why did all the women in his life have such horrible taste in men? He tiptoed through the living room to get to his room. He didn't want to have to talk to either his mother or Martin, so best not to let either of them know he was inside. He slowly shut his bedroom door, and then collapsed on his unmade bed.

"Is that you, Dan?" Martin hollered.

Martin insisted on calling him Dan, which Daniel hated. Nobody called him Dan. That wasn't his name. He'd been named after the pastor they'd had when he was born. Though the man's name was technically also Daniel, everybody had called him Pastor Dan. So, as little Daniel grew up in that church, no one called him Dan because they already had a Dan. Pastor was Dan. Little Daniel was Daniel.

Easy for everyone. Until Martin, anyway. This was too complicated for him, apparently.

Thinking about Pastor Dan made Daniel sad. He rolled over and put his headphones on, trying to force the memories out of his head. He hadn't told anyone in Portland that he'd grown up in a homeless shelter, anyone except Ember, that is. But she hadn't judged him, hadn't poked fun or anything. She didn't talk about hers much, but Ember seemed to know a bit about bad parents.

Daniel didn't know which was a better example of terrible parenting: that his mother had let him spend the first twelve years of his life in a homeless shelter; or that four years ago, she'd yanked him out of the only home he'd ever known. Daniel bit his lip. It had been four years. It felt like a lot longer. That kid who had lived in a church and healed people with his prayers—that kid was an entirely different person. A naive freak. He barely remembered him. He certainly didn't recognize him.

Someone pounded on his bedroom door. He knew it was Martin. His mother would've just opened the door, which didn't have a lock. He turned his music up and squeezed his eyes shut. At least, in this apartment, he *had* a door. They'd moved five times since the shelter. This was only his second door.

Through his eyelids, Daniel could tell there was more light in his room and knew someone had opened the door. If it was Martin, he was furious. But he didn't open his eyes to see. He hoped whoever it was would think he was asleep.

A large hand grabbed his lower leg to shake him awake. Martin. Daniel yanked his leg away and opened his eyes. "What?"

"Get up!" Martin hollered. "Your mother told you to go to the Laundromat!"

She hadn't told him any such thing. He pulled his headphones off and swung his legs off the bed. "I'll need money."

"It's in the laundry basket."

Daniel let out a long breath. He hated carrying his laundry down the street. It was embarrassing, and if he met any kids along the way, they always stared at him as he went by. But this, like everything else, had become his chore. His mother worked long hours as a waitress in a bar, so she thought Daniel should do all the chores. This was partly his fault. He'd established an expectation. When he was younger, he'd wanted to be helpful and had enjoyed making his mother happy. Now? Things had changed.

Chapter 3

Maggie

Maggie had just pulled her ancient car in front of the parsonage and shut her engine off when she heard the sirens. She didn't know where the emergency vehicles were headed, but as was her habit, she bowed her head and said a silent prayer for whoever was in crisis. When she picked her head up and opened her eyes, she saw the police cars pulling into her church's parking lot. *Oh no.*

She hurried out of the car and saw there was already a police officer standing beside the church building, with a dog on a leash. Had they tracked someone here? It wouldn't be the first time.

One of the cruisers pulled up beside her and came to a quick stop. An officer jumped out of the car, and she recognized him immediately: Ray Barlow. She greeted him by name and then waited for some sort of explanation.

"Have you seen Damien Foll?" he barked.

She shook her head. "No, not in weeks. He's not staying here anymore." She looked at the dog again. Was Damien back? What had he done?

"Go into your house, Maggie. He's armed." Apparently done with her, Barlow walked toward the back of the church. The other officers spread out around the building, and two went through the front door, with guns drawn. She realized that they were all wearing vests. The police came to their church all the time, but she didn't think they usually wore vests. Of course, these were the State Police, and Open Door Church more often dealt with the county sheriff's department. She looked around to see if any of the cars were county cruisers, but they weren't. State Police only. Whatever this was, it was serious.

She stood frozen to her spot, desperate for more information. Then she remembered that Isaiah was helping to paint one of the church's ceilings today, and she ran for the front door.

An officer stopped her before she got close.

She didn't know this one. "I have to go in. My son's in there." She tried to push past him, but he grabbed her arm. She yanked it away. "Let me go! I'm going in there! My son's in there!"

"I'm sorry, ma'am. You are *not* going in there."

"What are you going to do, arrest me?"

He tipped his head to the side and gave her a condescending look that said, yes, that's exactly what he would do if she didn't stop being ridiculous. She didn't know what to do, and the not knowing filled her eyes with tears. "What's going on?"

"Do you live here?"

"Yes," she said quickly. "Well, I live there." She nodded toward the parsonage. Despite herself, she was offended that he'd assumed she lived in the shelter. This was ridiculous, of course, because she had lived there once. "My husband is the pastor—"

The man's radio squawked, but Maggie couldn't understand what was said. "What was that? What is going on?"

"We're pursuing a suspect. Please go into your house and lock the door."

"What did he do?"

The officer gave her another patronizing glance.

"My son is in there! You have to tell me something!"

The front door flew open, and people spilled down the steps and into the parking lot. She scanned the faces, desperate to see her husband or her son, and grateful that her other son was at basketball camp. Isaiah saw her before she saw him and came running toward her. He hit her with such force, she had to step back to keep from falling over. She wrapped her arms around him and squeezed. "Are you okay?"

He pulled away from her and nodded. "Yeah. I'm fine. I don't even know what's going on. The police just told us there was a dangerous man in the shelter and for us to get out."

She looked at the large church in front of her. "Is Dad in there?"

Isaiah turned to look too. "Of course he is."

Her stomach rolled. "Why didn't he come out with the rest of you?"

Isaiah didn't answer her for several seconds. She stared at him, waiting. "I don't know, Mom," he finally said. Looking at her son in profile, his jaw tight, his arms folded across his chest, she was amazed at how much he looked like a younger version of his father. Her heart swelled with affection for them both, and part of her ached for that younger version of her husband, the man who had loved her so much back then.

The officer's radio squawked again, and though Maggie still couldn't make out most of the words, she did hear a request for an ambulance.

Chapter 4

Galen

Every muscle in Galen's body cried out in protest when he threw his body at Damien. On his way, he thought he heard sirens, but he wondered if it was his imagination. His mind felt thick and clunky, and he didn't trust his own thoughts. He slammed into Damien's small frame, using one arm to push Damien's gun hand toward the floor.

They crashed into the bunk beds and ricocheted. For a second, Galen worried they would both fall backward and Damien would end up on top of him, but he twisted his body and forced them to fall to his left, as far from Traci as possible.

The gun did not go off, but Damien still had an unworldly grip on the thing. Galen scrambled to his knees and grabbed Damien's arm. He pointed the gun toward the wall and violently shook his arm until finally, the gun fell loose. Galen extended one slow leg and kicked it away from them, and it skittered across the floor and under the bed. Galen gasped for air. He couldn't believe how slowly he was moving. It was like trying to swim in a tank of corn syrup.

He was vaguely aware that Traci had gone the rest of the way to the floor, as though she were bowing to the tangle of limbs that Damien and he currently were. Then little Justin got up and ran to his mother, who sat up to wrap her arms around him and pull him close. She spun away from them, keeping her body between the gunman and her son, murmuring comforting words into her son's hair.

Yes, those were definitely sirens. Thank God. Galen realized he should have prayed back when he had first seen the situation. And he should've prayed before making his move. He prayed now, an apology, followed by two requests: that he get Damien pinned and that the police move fast. As an afterthought, he also asked God to lessen the pain in his chest.

He was trying to force Damien onto his stomach, but the man wasn't making it easy. The twenty-something-year-old was stronger than he looked, or Galen was weaker than he thought. Damien was wiry, and his thrashing movements were illogical and unpredictable. At one point, Galen thought he had him pinned, but then Damien squirted free and almost made it to his feet. Galen grabbed one of his feet and yanked him back down to the floor. Damien cried out in pain, and Galen was glad that he'd hurt him. If Galen was going to be in so much pain, he wanted company.

Finally, Galen got the man onto his stomach and then straddled him. "Stop it," he said, breathing hard, too hard. "I don't want to hurt you." This wasn't entirely true, but he was trying to sound pastor-like.

Damien did not stop thrashing. He kicked both legs and arched his back like an angry bull in a rodeo. But he did not buck Galen off, nor was he going to. Galen had at least fifty pounds on him. Galen held the man's wrists with both hands and tried to catch his breath, but he couldn't. And the pain in his chest had returned. Or had it never left? He wasn't sure. It had all happened so fast. He was grateful for the miracle of adrenaline, but he wished he had a little more to get him through the next few minutes.

"Do you have a phone?" He could barely push the words out. He sounded like Methuselah.

"Yeah," Traci answered and got to her feet, not letting go of her son.

"Call 911. My phone's in my pocket, but I don't want to let go of him to reach for it."

Damien's thrashing increased in response. How was he not exhausted?

"I think the cops are already here," Galen said, "but you can tell them where in the building we are."

He heard footsteps in the hallway and hoped, if it wasn't the police, that it would at least be someone strong, someone who could help without sucking wind. He looked up at the open doorway and almost cried with relief when he saw the man who filled the doorway was clothed in blues. Galen leaned back, but his body leaned further than he'd told it to. The ceiling looked dark, too dark, and then Galen was falling, falling, knowing he should've hit the floor by now.

Chapter 5

Maggie

Maggie stood in the parking lot with her son and an assortment of church guests and watched the police bring Damien out in handcuffs. She hardly recognized him, though it had only been a few weeks since she'd seen him. He'd lost weight, and he looked pale.

"Whoa," Isaiah said, "he's been using something."

Maggie slid her arm around her son's waist and stared at the door, waiting for her husband to come out.

A man from Somalia who had been staying with them for a few weeks said something she didn't understand.

"Did you see what happened, Keem?" His name was Abdihakim, but someone at the church had started calling him Keem and she'd followed suit so she wouldn't keep butchering his full name. He said something else she didn't understand. He did appear to know something about what was going on, at least more than she did, but he wasn't able to explain it to her.

Galen still hadn't appeared, but she wasn't concerned. She figured he was chatting with the cops or working to comfort whatever guests were still inside. She wished she were still standing close enough to an officer to hear something over a walkie talkie, even if she could only make out some of the words.

When the ambulance pulled in with lights and siren, she still didn't worry about Galen. She assumed a guest had been hurt and looked around the parking lot to try to determine who was missing. Traci and Justin. They weren't outside yet. Her stomach fell. She watched the EMTs hurry up the church steps and mumbled a prayer for whomever it was they were going to help. She really hoped Justin hadn't been hurt. He was so little.

She was starting to lose her patience with the whole ordeal when the EMTs reappeared with a stretcher. It took her a few seconds to realize that the person strapped onto that stretcher was her husband. A primal cry erupted out of her, and she let go of Isaiah to run toward the small bed. Part of her knew that her son was right behind her.

The version of her husband that she saw as she drew closer did not comfort her. His skin was pasty, his hair was wet with sweat, and they were piping oxygen into his nose. She reached for his arm, sidestepping as the gurney continued to roll. His eyelids fluttered open. He looked at her, but she wasn't confident he'd seen her, and his lids fell again. His bare chest was covered with electrodes and wires. Did this mean he was having a heart attack? Or had Damien done something to him? "What happened? What's wrong with him?" Her voice didn't sound like hers.

"He's had a heart attack, ma'am," Joel said.

She tore her eyes away from Galen's face to look at the EMT she'd known for years. He knew her name. Why had he called her ma'am? This scared her more than anything else had. She tried to hold back a sob and almost succeeded. Was Galen going to die? She didn't know if she could survive that. "Is he going to be okay?"

They reached the ambulance.

"Tell me he's going to be okay." Sounding more like herself now.

Joel looked at her with soft eyes as his hands kept working. "We're going to get him to the hospital as fast as we can. Do you want to ride with us?" His expression suggested this was against the rules, but that he was going to allow it anyway. Did he think Galen was going to die on the way to the hospital?

She nodded and let go of Galen's arm so they could hoist him into the vehicle. Then Joel offered her a hand to help her up and in.

She'd hardly settled onto the bench seat before the ambulance was moving, and she wondered how Joel had moved so fast.

The church was only a few miles from the hospital. Galen was going to be okay, she told herself.

She looked at the paramedic sitting on the other side of Galen. She thought his name was Adam. He plugged Galen's oxygen tube into the ceiling of the ambulance and then got busy inserting an IV. She had a million questions for Adam, but he was busy, and obviously concentrating. She didn't want to interrupt his care of Galen. He spent a lot of time fiddling with his phone, and briefly, Maggie was annoyed by this, but then she realized he was using his phone to communicate with the hospital. She remembered then that she'd left Isaiah standing alone in the parking lot. She quickly texted him, told him to go inside, that she'd call him when she knew something. She wished she could think of an adult she could trust to bring him to the hospital, but she couldn't.

Slowly, giving Adam time to stop her if he needed to, she took Galen's hand into her own. His eyes opened but then quickly closed again, as if his eyelids were too heavy to hold up. His lips moved a little, but no sound came out.

"You can talk to him," Adam said without looking at her.

An Everest-sized lump took over her throat. She had infinite words she wanted to say to her husband. She couldn't think of a one. Especially not under these circumstances, with this audience. So she stayed quiet, wishing she could do better, wishing she could think of something beautiful to say, something to make Galen want to fight for his life, to want to stay with her.

Chapter 6

Galen

It was well after sundown when Galen finally started to feel like himself, finally started to think he might live through this ordeal. Doctors and nurses had been buzzing around him for hours, poking and drugging him and doing tests. He'd heard lots of words he didn't understand and many that he did: "heart attack," "resuscitate," "lucky to be alive."

After much ado, they put him in a quieter room with normal lighting that he appreciated. The lights were still bright, but they were so much softer than all the previous hospital lights had been, they felt almost dim. He was thrilled. A nurse helped him into his new bed and told him to sit tight for a moment. The implication was that he was to wait for something, but he had no idea what he was waiting for. He hoped it wasn't more tests.

Then a doctor appeared with his wife in tow, and his whole body relaxed at the sight of her. She looked so beautiful, as stunning as the first day he'd seen her. His friends, back when he'd had time for friends, had poked fun at him for claiming love at first sight—but it had been. He'd loved her that first second and he'd loved her every second since. She stopped approaching him and gave him a small smile. He wished she'd keep coming so he could reach her from the bed. He wanted to touch her. "Hi, honey. How are you?"

She laughed, and her eyes filled with tears. "How am I? I don't know, scared to death, grateful you're alive, somewhere in between. How are you?"

He felt like an idiot. He hadn't even thought about how scared she must have been through all this, was even a little surprised that she cared that much. "I'm sorry. How are the boys? They okay?"

She nodded, and her hair bounced. "They are good. They're just trusting God." She let out a single-syllable laugh. "Elijah keeps saying that God won't let you die because then there would be no one to run the shelter." They exchanged a sad, knowing look. Galen's predecessor, Pastor Dan, had died abruptly, leaving no one at his helm. And the church had almost sunk.

The doctor interrupted their telepathy session. "I'm Dr. Groshut, a cardiologist here at the hospital. I've just come on shift, and I've been looking over your information. Looks like I have both good news and not so good news."

Galen tore his eyes away from his wife's so he could look at the doc. "What's the not so good news?"

"The good news is," he said, ignoring Galen's preferred order of business as he consulted his clipboard, "that all your tests look good." He looked up, as if waiting for a celebration.

Galen didn't provide him with one. He was still waiting for the bad news.

"The bad news is, we're not entirely sure what caused your sudden cardiac arrest."

He frowned, not quite following. "Sudden cardiac arrest?"

Maggie stepped closer. "Your heart stopped. You basically died." Her eyes seemed to be asking him a question, but he didn't know what it was.

"Sorry," he said again.

"No need to be sorry," Dr. Groshut said. "You didn't intentionally stop your heart. But I would—"

"How am I alive?" he interrupted.

"One of the police officers brought you back. He had to shock your heart."

Galen's hand drifted to his chest. He'd died. His heart had called it quits. And then it had been shocked back to life. He couldn't wrap his mind around it.

"As I was saying, I would like to know what caused the event, so we can work to prevent a recurrence. As you know, we've done tests …"

Galen only sort of knew this. He remembered some things, but he'd been so tired. He looked at Maggie and saw fear in her eyes and wished he knew how to take that fear away. Though the doctor had been right—Galen hadn't done this on purpose—he still felt guilty. He suddenly missed his boys and wished they were there.

He realized the doctor was still talking. "… your EKG suggests you've had heart attacks in the past, but you told another physician that you weren't treated for them?"

Galen felt sick to his stomach. He'd had heart attacks? As in more than one? How could he have not known that?

Maggie stepped in. "No, he's never been treated for anything. We didn't know he had any heart problems." She looked at Galen. "He's been so busy, he probably wouldn't have noticed a heart attack." She delivered the words in monotone, but was there an extra layer of meaning hovering under her words?

Was she angry with him? Or was his irrational guilt making him imagine things?

No, he didn't think he was imagining it. "I didn't ask to be this busy," he said, and instantly wished he hadn't.

She pressed her lips into a tight line.

He looked away.

The doctor was talking again. "You likely had a heart attack immediately prior to your arrest. Did you have any chest pains or shortness of breath?"

Of course he had. He nodded slowly. And he'd been having chest pains for days. Weeks. He couldn't remember when they'd started.

"And your blood pressure is extremely high. Has this been going on for a while?"

He had no idea. He had no idea about any of this, and he wished the conversation would end. "Just tell me how to get better, Doc."

The doctor slowly shook his head. "We really can't say until we know what led us here. Have you been under any stress lately?"

Maggie barked out a laugh and both men looked at her. Then she looked embarrassed. "Sorry, it's just that he's under more stress than anyone I've ever known, and it's been going on for *years*." Her expression sobered. "Maybe this shouldn't be such a surprise."

"Maybe not," Dr. Groshut said. "And maybe that's one of the things we need to do. Work on reducing your stress load."

Galen wasn't going to argue with the man, but he didn't see how that was possible.

Chapter 7

Daniel

Daniel was sound asleep on the couch when something tapped on his window. His first reaction was fear, but then reason came to his rescue. The likelihood of someone or something menacing hanging out on his fire escape was low enough. The likelihood of this someone or something tapping on the window? He was safe.

He opened his eyes and looked at the window. She was backlit by the city lights, but there was no mistaking that profile. It was Ember, with her hair up in a sloppy bun secured with a giant scrunchy. He swung his legs off the couch and tiptoed to the window.

It creaked when he opened it, and he stopped, bracing himself for a reaction from his mom's room, which she shared with Martin. Martin was a light sleeper. Daniel had been caught a few times trying to sneak out. Of course, he'd used the door. Apparently, he should've used the window because this hadn't woken Martin up. Daniel exhaled and opened the window the rest of the way. "What are you doing?" he whispered so quietly he almost couldn't hear himself.

She giggled loudly.

He would've waved at her to shush but he was helping her climb through the window so he only said, "Shh."

She stood up straight and smiled at him. Then kissed him on the cheek. "Why are you sleeping on the couch?" she whispered, but he could only think about the kiss.

He took her hand and pulled her toward his bedroom, knowing that she knew him well enough not to get the wrong idea. He closed the door behind them. "We can't wake up Martin."

"I know," she said and giggled again.

This was far too much giggling. "Are you high?"

She leaned into him. "Maybe?"

Ah, that explained the kiss on the cheek. "Okay. Why are you here?"

She faked a pout. "Because you're my best friend"—she took his hand—"and I wanted to see my best friend."

She was lying. Not about the best friend part. But she had another reason to be there. She sat on the end of his bed and then fell back with her arms spread wide. "Why were you sleeping on the couch?"

How was that so interesting to her? He sat down beside her but refrained from falling back as she had. "I sleep there a lot. It's hard for me to fall asleep. Helps to watch TV until I do."

"Oh. I see." She drew out the word *see* for too long and then giggled again. She put a hand on his back. "I'm going to hang out here for a minute, okay?"

Yes, this was okay with him. "Okay, but my door doesn't lock, and if Martin catches us, he's going to have a fit."

She sat up abruptly, her face etched with concern so extreme it looked fake. He knew it wasn't. "Does Martin hit you?"

He shook his head quickly. "No, thank God. He just rants and raves and never shuts up."

She leaned into him and put her head on his shoulder. He looked away to keep from kissing her. "The last guy hit you, right?"

She knew this. Why was she bringing it up now? Because she was high. "Yeah, the last guy did all sorts of stuff. So, who were you partying with tonight?"

"Partying?" She tried to feign innocence.

He raised his eyebrows to call her bluff.

She shrugged and kicked her feet like she was dangling them off the side of a pool instead of off the side of his bed. She studied her fascinating toes. "I wasn't partying. It was just me and mum."

He knew her mom shared drugs with her sometimes, so he didn't need to ask for clarification. It was the only time they got along. "Did she pass out?"

"No." Her feet stopped moving and all giggle had left her voice. Something had happened. He wanted to pry, but he didn't. She looked at him, digging her chin into her shoulder. "Her stupid boyfriend showed up and she was done hanging out with me. What about you?"

"What about me?"

"You ever party with your mom?"

He laughed too loudly. That was ridiculous. "Never."

"Why not? She parties, right?" She was almost mewing.

"Uh …" Where was she going with this? "Sometimes. Not much." *Not as much as your mom*, he almost said.

"So, does she have any stuff around?"

Yep, that's what he'd been afraid of. "So you only came over here because your mom stopped giving you stuff?" His hands closed into fists.

"No, no, no!" She reached out and put her hands on his cheeks and for a second he

34

thought she was going to kiss him, to *really* kiss him this time—but she didn't. She dropped her hands and said, "I'm sorry," in a voice that finally sounded like hers. "I'm just so miserable." She put her hands over her face and started rubbing so hard he was afraid she'd hurt herself. "I just want something, need something, to make me numb." She looked up at him. "You know?"

He did know that feeling. He knew it well. "Yep."

She leaned away from him, giving him a cutting look. "No, you don't, Mr. Goody Two Shoes. Mr. Grew Up in a Church. You never get in trouble."

This wasn't true. He just didn't get into trouble on as grand a scale as she did. "That's the first time you've ever made fun of me for growing up in a homeless shelter."

She groaned. "I didn't make fun of you for living in a homeless shelter. I made fun of you for living in a *church*." She emphasized the last word with far too much volume.

"Ember! You have to be quiet or I'm going to throw you out."

"No, you won't."

She was right. She flopped back onto the bed again and patted the tangle of blankets. "Lie down beside me."

Against his better judgment, he did, leaving a buffer of a few inches between them. Not because he didn't trust her, but because he didn't trust himself. They lay like that for several minutes, the lower half of their legs still hanging off the end of the bed. Daniel's feet hit the floor. Hers did not. She was petite.

"What was it like?"

He hesitated. "What was what like?"

"The church. What was it like growing up in a church?" She rolled onto her side and propped her head up with her elbow, studying him. "Who is Daniel Holland?"

Daniel couldn't stand her gaze and returned his eyes to the ceiling. He had no idea who he was.

She poked him in the ribs. "I'm serious. Tell me."

He closed his eyes. Was he really going to do this? Part of him wanted to open up to her. Part of him was working very hard to figure out a way to change the subject. "I don't know. It was a church."

"But I don't know what that's like, so you have to explain it to me."

"Well …" He took a deep breath. Yes, he was really going to do this. It felt a little like jumping off a cliff, except that it also felt like stepping into a warm room after a long time outside in January. "It was actually kind of awesome. My pastor was like my dad. He sort of adopted me, but he wasn't with my mom or anything. He taught me about God and he took me fishing—"

"Do you still believe in all that?"

He looked at her. "Believe in fishing?"

She laughed. "No, silly. In God."

He returned his gaze upward. "I don't know. Sometimes."

"Why don't you?" Her words were measured.

She was being so serious! He'd never seen this side of her before. Despite the fact that he'd pretty much decided to be an atheist, he still didn't dare say it out loud. "I just figure … well, I was a good kid. I mean a *really* good kid, a little warrior for Jesus." He decided now wasn't the time to tell her how he'd healed a couple dozen people with his prayers. "So, I don't think a real God would let my mother take me away from there and put me in a place with Floyd." He could hardly bring himself to say the monster's name. "So if God is real, then he certainly doesn't love me, and if he doesn't love a kid like I used to be, then what's the point?"

She didn't say anything at first. Then she rolled toward him, swung her arm over his stomach, and rested her head on his shoulder. "I'm sorry you had to go through all that with Floyd."

He tentatively wrapped one arm around her and gently rested his free hand on her forearm. "Yeah. I'm sorry too."

Chapter 8

Ember

Daniel had fallen asleep. Ember knew she should leave. She may or may not get caught sneaking back into her apartment, but if she was going to get caught, the sooner the better. Sneaking in at three in the morning was much worse than sneaking in at one. But she couldn't make herself move.

Slowly, so as not to wake him, she turned her head to look at Daniel. The soft light fell through the window and lit up his profile. He was so handsome. She didn't deserve his friendship, let alone more. She knew how he felt about her, and she felt the same about him. But it didn't matter. She could never be with him.

She turned her eyes back toward the ceiling and fought against tears. This stupid life. So often she wanted it to end. If she couldn't end the painful parts, then she'd just as soon end it all. What was the point of any of it? Daniel was the only person on the planet who cared about her, and if he knew who she really was, what she'd really *done*, then he wouldn't love her anymore. He'd be disgusted by her.

She should probably walk away from him altogether, before he did find everything out, before they both got hurt. But she needed him. He was the only thing keeping her sane. Or close to sane, anyway.

She let out a long breath and then forced herself to slide out from under Daniel's arm. She didn't want to leave. She had to leave.

She climbed out onto the fire escape and paused to let the ocean breeze dry her tears. It felt good on her cheeks, almost refreshing. Not refreshing enough.

She used her key to let herself through the front door of her apartment building and then crept up the stairs. She could hear voices before she reached her door and knew she was busted, but she tried to be sneaky anyway. She opened the door just wide enough to slip through. She looked around. The voices she'd heard had come from the television. She tiptoed toward her room.

"Where've you been?" her mother called from the couch. She said something else too, but Ember couldn't make it out. It was just as well. Her words were never worth hearing.

She continued toward her room.

"Come-ere!"

She considered ignoring the instruction, but it would lead to more drama, so she went to her mother. She rounded the corner to find her disheveled mother's face lit by the television's glow, her feet propped up on her boyfriend-of-the-week's lap. He was passed out. "You just missed your uncle," her mother said. "Hand me my cigarettes."

The mention of her uncle was a fist to her stomach—physical pain as well as sickness. The menthols were well within her mother's reach, but Ember handed them to her anyway.

"He wanted to see you."

I'm sure he did. "I'm going to bed now." She walked away, nearly choking on her hatred. Her mother was a monster. All Ember's life, she'd been making excuses for her mother, but she was done. She had told her mother a year ago what her uncle was doing, and her mother had slapped her and called her a liar. Now he shows up in the middle of the night looking for her and that didn't tell her mother anything?

Her mother knew the truth. Either she was refusing to deal with it or she didn't care. Or both. Probably both.

Ember slammed her bedroom door and sat on the edge of her bed. She should've stayed with Daniel. Here, it was too easy to remember who she really was. She glanced behind her at the tangle of dirty sheets on her bed and decided she'd rather lie on the floor. So she did.

It was hard and uncomfortable, but she knew she deserved it. She probably deserved worse. This was stupid. Sticking around in this world was stupid. She needed to figure out a way to escape. Whatever it took. This vague notion of freedom comforted her enough so she was able to drift off to sleep—a sleep crowded with nightmares.

Chapter 9

Maggie

Brilliant morning sunlight shone through the hospital window in narrow shafts.

"You didn't have to kick the boys out." Galen looked better. He'd finally gotten some sleep and was starting to look and act like his old self.

She chuckled and pulled a chair closer to his bed. "I didn't *kick* them out. I just sent them on a wild goose chase so that we could have a few minutes to talk."

He raised an eyebrow. "I've never heard anyone call tapioca pudding a wild goose."

She chuckled again, this time with more sincerity. "You're right. It probably won't take them long to locate the pudding, so we should talk quickly."

"Okay. What do you want to talk about?"

She took a deep breath and let it out slowly. She wanted to talk about a million things. *One thing at a time*, she told herself. "I'm wondering if we should walk away from Open Door."

As she'd predicted, his mouth fell open in surprise. Apparently, he'd never considered this before. "That might be a little extreme."

She waited a few seconds. "Is it, though?"

He stared at her, and she willed herself to be patient. Give him time to process.

"Honey, the place would shut down. Isn't this why everybody begged me to take the job after Dan died? To keep it from shutting down? How are things different now than they were then?"

Her patience was dissipating. "Because you've given them *eight years!*" she said quickly.

He leaned his head back against his pillow and closed his eyes. "Yes, I have," he said softly. "But that doesn't mean I can stop."

"Why not?"

He popped one eye open and peered at her. "You been thinking about this for longer than the last two days?"

Uh oh. Busted. "Not necessarily, but you really scared me yesterday. I don't want to lose you. I know you are committed to the church and to your people, but I don't want—"

"*My* people?" he interrupted.

What did he mean? "Yeah."

"You used to say *our* people."

"Oh, whatever. Then *our* people. I still cut their hair, don't I?" And the truth was, she'd grown mightily sick of it. "My point is, I think we should consider starting a new chapter in our lives, and if that means that the church shuts down, then so be it. I don't mean to be cold, but Galen, we've done our time. If God wants to keep the church open, he'll keep it open, just like he did the last time that church lost a pastor."

Galen stared at her as if she was speaking a foreign language. This wasn't going as well as she'd hoped. "Aren't you worried about disobeying God?" He said it gently, without an ounce of judgment.

She'd known this point was coming, and she was ready. She leaned forward and rested her elbows on her knees. "Are you sure God still wants you doing this? Has he told you that lately?"

Galen's expression changed. She'd finally broken through—one layer at least.

"I'm not saying we don't pray about it. I'm saying we do, but I've been praying about it for a while now, and I think God is trying to set us free."

He furrowed his brows. "He gave me a heart attack to set me free?"

"I'm not saying that, but ... will you just pray? Just consider it? Don't we get to have a happy season in life?"

His eyes fell. Oh no, she'd pushed too far. "You haven't been happy?" he said, his voice low.

"No, no, I'm not saying that. I wouldn't trade my life with you and the boys for anything." She stopped, trying to figure out how to say what she was feeling. "But I'm *tired*. And ... and ... I *miss you*."

He gave her the tenderest look then, a look that rewound years. His love for her was still in there somewhere. She'd just seen it in his eyes. "Honey, I didn't—" he started.

"Yoo-hoo!" Someone called from the doorway, and Maggie didn't think she'd ever been so annoyed. She turned to see a couple enter the room, and it took her a second to identify who they were. In fact, it wasn't until the woman wrapped her arms around her that it clicked into place: Pastors Steven and Jill Udi, from Lewiston.

Chapter 10

Galen

Galen was annoyed that Steven and Jill had interrupted his conversation with Maggie, the first real one they'd had in he-didn't-know-how-long that didn't involve how to get someone a bus ticket from Portland, how to make enough spaghetti for fifty people with three tomatoes, or how to get rid of bedbugs. But he was also thrilled to see them. If anyone could understand what had driven his heart to demand a vacation, it was these two: the pastors of the homeless shelter church in Lewiston.

He accepted Steven's handshake. "You guys didn't have to come all the way up here."

"Are you kidding?" Steven looked around for a chair. "I wanted to just call and send flowers, but Jill here demanded that we come in person to tell you we care."

Galen was touched. "Well, I thank you. That's very kind of you."

"Not too kind." He finally found a chair and dragged it across the room. "I wanted to bring you some good food, but Jill wouldn't let me."

Jill remained standing. "I didn't know what was going on with you health-wise, and didn't want to interfere with any diet they might have you on."

Steven rolled his eyes, but Galen thought that if Jill could see Steven's eyes, he might not have been so bold with the rolling. "Anyway, what *did* happen to you, friend? You're too young to be having heart attacks."

"I'm older than I look," Galen said, trying to be funny.

No one laughed.

"But honestly, we don't know what caused it. My heart just decided to take a break. A police officer happened to be on the scene because we had a cop-shooting suspect in our church, and he zapped my heart back into action."

"Yeah, we heard about that," Steven said. "So sad. The news said he was hiding out in your shelter?"

No one answered him.

"Did you guys know the cop who was killed? I think they said his name was Klaus?"

"Yes," Maggie said. "Deputy Ben Klaus. He was a nice man."

Galen closed his eyes. It was too much. "He was so young. And I think he had a young son."

Maggie nodded. "Yes, John is four."

"So sad," Steven said again. "Is that what caused your heart attack? Having a man in your church waving a gun around?"

Galen shrugged. "I don't know. I certainly overexerted myself wrestling a younger man to the floor, but I think my trouble was already brewing." It was hard to admit how foolish he'd been. "I'd been having chest pains for a while, and I've been beyond exhausted these last few months." *Few months* was probably an understatement. He couldn't remember feeling rested.

"And you didn't go to the doctor?" Jill asked.

He was suddenly irrationally annoyed with her skirt suit and her thick makeup. He looked at his wife's flawless skin and had the urge to caress her cheek. Too bad she was eight feet away. "No, I didn't go to the doctor. I planned on getting to it eventually, but, as I'm sure you can understand, someone else always had a more pressing crisis."

Steven and Jill exchanged a look. "But you need to make time for yourself," Steven said. "Get someone to cover for you so you can take care of business."

Galen's laugh sounded more contemptuous than he'd intended. "Sorry, but get *who* to cover for me? My only option is my poor wife

49

and I hate leaving her there alone without backup."

"Your wife?" Steven exclaimed. "Don't your members serve in the shelter?"

Galen gave Maggie an incredulous look and then returned his gaze to his friend. "What members?"

Steven hesitated, confused, and then laughed. "What do you mean? The members! The people who go to your church on Sundays, the people who worship with you and tithe with you, and I would hope, *serve* with you."

Galen had started shaking his head before Steven finished his sentence. "We don't have any of those."

Steven looked horrified. "Why not? Where did they all go?"

Galen closed his eyes as if that would help him remember. "We never had more than a half dozen, and slowly, those have just moved on." He opened his eyes. "It's exhausting. They got tired."

"Of course they got tired if there were only six of them!" He looked at Jill. "They need a revival!"

The word sent an unexpected shiver up Galen's spine. Yes. That's exactly what they needed, but revivals happened to other people in other places. They didn't happen in homeless shelters in Mattawooptock, Maine.

"Revival?" Maggie said. Galen knew that she understood the word, and that her question was really, "Do you really think that's possible?"

But Steven misunderstood her. "Yes! Revival! You put up a big tent"—Maggie covered a snicker with one hand—"and you invite a band or two to play some good old rockin' tunes and you share the Gospel and you give a few rousin' altar calls and then *bam!* you've got people excited about Jesus again." He shook his fist in the air. "You've got to rally the troops! Do it on a different property, though, so you're not associating it with the shelter."

First, Galen thought this whole idea sounded ridiculous. Second, he thought that even if he could manage to pull it off, the newly excited people would just go to other churches.

"I don't think we could afford a tent," Maggie said, sounding as cynical as Galen felt.

"If you can't afford a tent, you need more tithers," Steven said.

If they had more tithers, Galen thought, they would do a lot of things before they would invest in a rental tent.

"We'll rent a tent for you!" Steven exclaimed.

Galen didn't want to do this. He wanted nothing to do with this. "Thank you for the suggestion, and thank you for the generous offer." He had no idea how much a tent cost, but he assumed it was a lot. "But I don't think Mattawooptock citizens are unexcited about Jesus. We've got lots of active churches with lots of active ministries. We just don't have anyone at *our church*." Galen hated talking about this. It had bothered him for years, and on some level, he'd always felt it must be his fault. He wasn't a good enough preacher. He wasn't a good enough evangelist. He couldn't miraculously heal anyone. Several years ago, they'd had many helpful members. He'd been one of them. Then Dan had died, he'd taken over, and slowly, the congregation had trickled away, leaving only homeless people behind. "I mean, we have lots of homeless people," he added. "They help some."

Steven was thinking. Galen wished he wouldn't. He didn't want any more bad ideas thrown at him.

"I wonder if it's because your shelter is your church," Jill offered.

Huh? What did that mean?

"Yeah." Steven nodded. He apparently spoke Jill.

Galen wondered if he was going to translate.

"See, our shelter is a separate building," Steven said. "People walk from the shelter to the church for services and Bible studies, but they don't actually *live* in the church."

"What difference does that make?" Maggie asked, managing to sound petulant.

Galen almost laughed. She never sounded like that, and it was cute.

Steven shrugged. "I don't know. Maybe it doesn't make any difference. But we've got a thousand members who don't live in our shelter." He said this without an ounce of smugness. "So maybe that separation makes the church more comfortable to members." He sounded as though he was figuring this out for the first time. "Maybe it makes us more approachable to new people."

Galen could see his point. "I'm not remodeling our church to make non-homeless people more comfortable."

Steven nodded. "Okay then. I suggest you put up a tent."

Chapter 11

Galen

They'd released Galen from the hospital, but his wife wouldn't let him into the church. She'd been bouncing from church to parsonage and back, telling everyone in the church that she was his proxy, and then coming to him when she needed advice. But there weren't many crises because there weren't many people. The weather had been gorgeous, and not many were staying at the shelter.

She reported back that Harry was giving her some trouble but told Galen not to worry about him. She could handle Harry.

It didn't matter how nice the weather was— Harry would be at the shelter. Harry had set a record for the longest shelter stay: seven and a half years. And he showed no signs of moving on.

It wasn't that Harry loved living in a homeless shelter. He didn't. He complained about it all the time, and his complaints were justified. It wasn't easy living there. The food was usually terrible, the Bible studies were mandatory, and they had recurring bedbug breakouts. And there were a lot of people there. Obnoxious people. Inconsiderate people. Loud people. Smelly people.

Still, he remained.

At least he was helpful. He was currently the sole member of the worship team. In the past, they'd had so many musicians eager to serve that they'd rotated teams through the schedule, ending up with great live music for every Bible study and every service. Now they just had one sad old man with one sad old guitar.

And when Harry was in the mood, he helped Maggie out in the office. When he wasn't in the mood, he hid in his room and drank. He thought he was hiding the drinking from Galen, but he wasn't. Galen was just choosing his battles. Though, as a single man, Harry should have lived in the large men's bunkroom with the rest of the single men, he'd long ago moved into a private bedroom one summer when the shelter was almost empty. As the weather cooled and the shelter filled up, Harry refused to move back to the big room. Again, Galen did not choose that particular battle.

Galen had been counseling Harry since a few weeks after he'd first arrived on Open Door's doorstep. Back then, Galen had repeatedly gotten his hopes up only to have them dashed by Harry's unwillingness to step out. Over and over, Galen had found him housing options and job options, and Harry would light up when hearing about them, but then wouldn't send the resume, or wouldn't fill out the online form, or wouldn't show up for the interview. Once, Galen had tried to physically force Harry out of the church and into his truck so he could take him to an open apartment he'd been approved for.

But Harry wouldn't go. Galen could still remember the look on his face. Harry had been terrified.

Galen genuinely liked Harry, but sitting alone in his living room, Galen was grateful for a break from him.

The first few hours of Galen's forced vacation, he'd enjoyed spending time on his couch, enjoyed watching television. But now he was growing bored. He was still staring at the old western on the screen, but his mind was in a dozen different places. Should he really consider his wife's suggestion that they quit serving at Open Door? He'd prayed about it a lot, but hadn't received any divine direction, leaving him to spend too much time and effort mentally wrestling with the question himself. Did he really need to put up a tent? He wasn't a great speaker and couldn't picture himself drawing crowds with his dynamic sermons. But would it work? He trusted the Udis. They had been running a shelter for years and had a huge, happy congregation, so they obviously knew what they were doing. He didn't want to ask them to pay for the tent, though.

He muted the Wild West saloon scene and bowed his head. "Father," he started. And then he got stuck. This was unusual. Galen prayed all the time, but he only had two types of prayers in his arsenal: the morning prayers, which were long lists fired off rapidly so he could get to his day; and quick spurts of prayer in the middle of chaos.

Right now, his house felt uncomfortably calm and quiet. He took a breath and tried to start again, but it was hard to find the words. He decided to simplify. "I don't know what you want, and I want to know what you want. I want to do what you want." He took another deep breath and he felt his whole body relax; he was suddenly more relaxed than he'd been in months. Maybe quiet, calm prayers were good for his blood pressure. "And God, if you want me to put up a tent, please let me know. In Jesus' name, I pray. Amen."

He opened his eyes and looked at the screen, but he was so relaxed that he figured he'd better capitalize on it, so he rolled over and pulled the blanket up to his chin. He'd never been so ready for a nap.

Chapter 12

Galen

Galen woke up to Maggie shaking his shoulder. He looked over his shoulder at her and opened one eye. "What's up?" he asked, trying to hide the fact that he wasn't happy to have his nap ended prematurely.

"Sorry to wake you, but the police are here."

When he opened his eyes the rest of the way, he saw a man and a woman in matching gray suits standing behind his wife. A little embarrassed, he sat up, swinging his legs off the couch. Out of habit, he reached for his chest, expecting a pain that wasn't there. The new meds must be working. Or maybe it was the nap. "How can I help you?" He started to stand, but one of the suits held up a hand.

"Please, stay comfortable. We understand your condition." The male suit glanced sideways at Maggie, a look that suggested to Galen that she had tried to prevent this interview.

Galen was happy to remain on the couch. "Have a seat." He swung his arm across the room, and each detective took an armchair. He gave Maggie a look that said, *Maybe we should offer them a beverage or something*, but either Maggie didn't understand his silent message or ignored it. Probably the latter. He smiled at the man because he seemed to be in charge. The smile alone tired him out. Maybe he wasn't out of the woods yet. He ran a hand over his face, stopping to massage his jaw.

"Sorry to bother you, Mr. Turney. I'm Detective Buker. I believe we've met before."

Galen didn't remember this, but he nodded.

"And this is my partner, Detective Slaughter."

Galen almost winced at her name.

She gave him a tight smile.

"We just need to ask you a few questions about Damien Foll."

Galen nodded.

Detective Buker flipped open a small notebook. "Can you describe what you saw when you entered the room?"

Galen closed his eyes to think. He could remember the incident, but his memory looked more like a photo album than a movie, and he wasn't sure the photos were in chronological order. He cleared his throat. "It's a little foggy. I wasn't feeling well, but Damien had his back to me, and he was pointing a gun at Traci, who was on her knees, terrified." His stomach rolled at the memory. "Her little boy, Justin, was to my right, also kneeling." He stopped.

"And how did Foll seem?"

Foll? It seemed weird to be calling Damien by his last name. "He seemed ... frantic ... terrified."

"And what else?" Buker pressed.

What else? How did he know? "I don't know. I was mostly paying attention to the gun."

Buker nodded, seeming to relax his push a little.

Slaughter spoke for the first time. "Describe his body, his movements."

Buker gave her a scolding look, but Galen didn't know what she'd done wrong. Was she not allowed to talk?

Galen thought. "He was a little shaky, I guess, but like I said, I just thought he was scared. Oh wait, I do remember that his pupils were dilated."

Buker wrote that down. "Anything else?"

Galen wanted to go back to sleep. "Well, once I started wrestling with him, I thought he seemed too strong for his size, but now I think that was just because I was weaker than usual because of my heart."

"Yeah, you did a really good job defusing the situation," Buker said. "You're quite the local hero."

He was? He hadn't known anyone knew about what had happened. He looked at Maggie and she was beaming. He couldn't remember the last time she had looked proud of him. It was a great feeling. He couldn't stop looking at her.

"Did he say anything?" Slaughter asked.

Galen grudgingly pulled his eyes away from Maggie to look at Slaughter. "Just that he'd done a bad thing."

"He said that?" Buker and Slaughter said in unison.

Galen nodded and tried to think. "I think he said something else too, but I can't quite remember. I think he might have said, 'I think he's dead.'"

Buker hesitated. Galen suspected that neither detective was breathing and he wished he could give them more. "You *think* he said that, or he said it?"

Galen didn't know. "Are we sure he did this?"

"Do you find that hard to believe?"

Galen thought back over all he knew about Damien, which was precious little. "I don't know."

Buker nodded. Slaughter took out her own notebook and started scribbling.

"Did you smell anything weird?" Buker asked.

Galen scowled. "I don't think so."

"How about sounds? Hear anything unusual?"

"You mean from Damien?"

Buker shrugged. "Anything at all."

Galen was taking a test, and he was failing. What did they want him to say? "I thought I heard sirens at one point." He tried to be patient as he waited for the pop quiz to continue, glad his wife hadn't offered them a beverage.

Finally, Buker said, "Can you think of anything else? Anything at all?"

What else was there to say? "Traci said he came in through the window. Somehow, I gathered that he was trying to hide from someone, but found her and Justin in the way, so, in a panic, pointed his gun at her. I don't know why. He wasn't behaving rationally. I figured he was on drugs or something—"

Buker and Slaughter sighed in unison.

Finally. He'd said something that mattered.

Buker's notebook was open again. "What made you think he was on drugs?"

Hadn't he just told them that? "I don't know." This time, Galen failed to keep the impatience out of his voice. "Just the whole scene. He looked jittery, his pupils were huge, and why else would he be pointing a gun at Traci? Traci told me she didn't even know him. And then he told me he'd shot a cop."

"He said that?" Buker exclaimed. "He said he shot a cop?"

Galen squeezed his eyes shut, confused now, and wishing he'd stopped talking a long time ago. "No, not exactly. He said he thought someone was dead ... that he thought a cop was dead ... and I guess I assumed because he was waving a gun around—"

"He was waving the gun around?" Slaughter asked.

Speaking over her, Buker said, "Did he say he shot a cop or not?"

Galen didn't know. "I don't think so. But it was implied."

"Was he really waving the gun around?" Slaughter asked again.

"No," Galen said, annoyed. "It was just an expression. The only time the gun was waving around was when I was trying to get it away from him." He remembered then that the gun had been wobbling, as if it was too heavy for Damien, but he was tired of talking.

"So, let me make sure I get this right," Buker said. "Foll said, 'I think he's dead. I think the cop is dead.' And that's all he said?" Buker sounded disappointed.

Galen nodded. "I think so."

Buker snapped his notebook shut and stood. He pulled a card out of his pocket and handed it to Galen. "If you think of anything else, please give me a call, day or night."

Galen took the card and nodded again. "Sorry I couldn't be more help."

Buker's expression softened. "Oh, you've been plenty of help, Mr. Turney. You pinned a cop killer to the floor and held him there till we got here. You probably saved that young woman's life."

Galen didn't think Damien would have shot Traci, but then again, he didn't think he'd ever shoot Deputy Klaus either.

Buker and Slaughter were walking away.

"Do you know why he did it?"

Buker turned back. "He's saying he didn't, but Deputy Klaus had just pulled his car over. He didn't have a license, and we found his car full of drugs." Buker gave Galen a grave look, a curt nod, and then turned to go, and Maggie showed them both out.

Galen tipped over to lie back down and Maggie asked him if he wanted the mail.

"Sure." Why not?

Maggie brought him a pile of it. Bills, credit card offers, a letter from their sponsored child in the Dominican Republic, and a flyer from a brand-new business in Augusta—The Tent Shop, offering tent rentals of all sizes for all occasions.

Chapter 13

Maggie

"Honey?" Galen called from the living room.

"Hang on." She pulled his steaming chicken noodle soup out of the microwave. She would have been happy to make him the real, homemade stuff, but he preferred the canned version. She stuck a potholder under the bottom of the bowl, grabbed a spoon and a sleeve of Saltines, and headed his way.

He looked exhausted.

"I wish they hadn't come today. You still need your rest and that was stressful." She handed him the soup and spoon and then pulled a folding TV tray out of the corner.

He thanked her and gave her an annoyed look. "I'm not that fragile. That wasn't stressful."

If you say so. "Well, I don't know what they wanted you to say, or what they needed you to say." She got the table snapped into place and then handed him the crackers. "They've obviously got him dead to rights."

He set his bowl on the table. "I agree, but I should probably go see him in jail, or prison"— her stomach twisted in disbelief—"or wherever he is, in a few days." He blew on a spoonful, put it in his mouth, and then looked at her. "What? What's the matter?"

Should she tell him what was the matter? Or pretend nothing was the matter? She was so tired of him trying to minister to everyone, everywhere, at all times, but she didn't want to fight with him. But maybe if she'd said something a year or two ago, he never would have almost died.

He swallowed. "What?" he said again.

"Nothing." She sat down in the recliner Slaughter had recently vacated.

He reached toward the mail pile on the couch beside him. "You're not going to believe this." He handed her a one-page flyer.

"What is it?" she asked, but as soon as she looked at it, she knew what it was. Her eyes snapped up. "You can't be serious."

"Look, I *just* prayed about this. I mean, only a few hours ago. I told God I would put up a tent and hold a revival meeting if he wanted me to, and then I get this in the mail." He paused. "I think God wants me to do it."

She knew, beyond a shadow of a doubt, that God wanted no such thing. But how could she convince her husband of this? She considered her words carefully and decided to ask a question that she'd been wanting to ask for a while but hadn't because the idea scared her a little. "Remember when you got shot, and you saw Jesus?"

He chuckled and let go of his spoon. "Of course. Nobody forgets something like that."

She stared at him, trying to ask the question with her eyes.

His face fell. He understood. "No, not this time. And believe me, I've wondered why. Maybe I didn't really die this time. Maybe I only almost died."

She didn't think so. His heart had stopped. Wasn't that death? "Do you remember anything from that time?"

"You mean the time when my heart wasn't beating?"

She gave him a small nod.

"No, sorry. I remember seeing the cops and then waking up in the hospital."

She tried not to show her disappointment. She was sure that, if Galen would have seen Jesus again, Jesus would have told him to put the brakes on. Slow down a little.

"Why do you ask?"

"Just curious," she said quickly. "Anyway, I don't think we need to put up a tent. I think the Udis are crazy."

"Maggie, we're broke. The church is broke. Our family is broke. We could barely keep the heat on last winter and we eat canned beans far too often—"

"We just need to trust God," she interrupted.

"I do," he snapped. "Of course I do. I've been trusting God every step of the way since I said I'd take over as pastor, but I'm tired ..."

Relief washed over her at the sound of those words. He was admitting it!

"... and it would be nice to have some help around here, other than you and Harry. We are running ragged, and it almost killed me. Without a congregation, I'm not sure how much longer I'll last." He seemed pained to admit it.

"I know. But if our choices are stepping away or trying to attract an army to help us, don't you think stepping away would be easier?"

He hesitated. "I'm not going to let the shelter shut down. Where would all these people go?"

She didn't know the answer to that. But she also didn't care anymore. She just wanted her husband back. She wanted her boys' father back.

He pointed to the flyer. "I think God wants me to put up a tent."

She wanted to crumple the stupid flyer up and throw it across the room, but she didn't. She held it in her left hand and dropped her arm over the left side of the chair. "And I think that God wants no such thing."

Galen blinked, surprised at her boldness.

She was a little surprised herself, but this had been a long time coming. He had almost died. She needed to be stronger, do a better job of sticking up for him, if he wasn't going to do it himself.

"I think we should pray about it."

She rolled her eyes. "You don't think I've been praying about it?!"

He picked the TV tray up and set it aside. Then he slid toward the edge of the couch, and reached out with both hands. "I mean, I think we should pray together."

A lump formed in her throat as she scooched toward her husband and took his hands. It felt so good to feel his warm skin on hers. She couldn't remember the last time they'd prayed together. It had been years. She bowed her head in reverence to God, and also to keep her husband from seeing her tears.

And then the married couple prayed.

Chapter 14

Maggie

Feeling re-energized from her couple's prayer session, Maggie bounced into church ready to face come what may.

This supernatural energy was quickly expended. Jenessae and Traci had come to fisticuffs over some man Maggie didn't know, and Maggie had to decide whether to involve the police. She didn't want to, figured she'd already spent enough time with them for one day. And Harry figured out that they had no food for supper.

Not *almost no food*; that wouldn't have been unusual. Literally *no food.* Unless she counted the giant can of mandarin oranges that had expired the year before.

Normally, she'd have seen such a shortage coming, and responded accordingly, but she'd been a little distracted.

She stood beside Harry, staring into the pantry, at the paltry can of fruit.

"What are we going to do?" Harry asked.

Maggie held in a snide remark. Harry wasn't exactly wasting away to nothing. He could stand to fast for an evening. She mentally ran through the small catalog of food she had in the parsonage: a bag of salad that may or may not be wilted; some frozen pizza bites; a half a box of pancake mix; and some sheets of seaweed from the time that Isaiah had decided to be a sushi chef. She was creative, but even she couldn't make an edible combination out of those offerings. "I don't know," she said, partially to herself and partially to Harry. She looked up at him. "How many people are here right now?"

He shrugged. "I don't know, twenty or so?"

She didn't think there were that many, but she could be wrong. And it didn't matter if there were twenty people or eight. That can of mandarin oranges wasn't going to go far, and she knew what their checkbook register looked like. Galen would know what to do. He always knew what to do. But she didn't want to bother him. "Got any ideas?"

Harry guffawed. "Me?" He swore. "No."

She continued to stare at the oranges until she finally acquiesced that they weren't going to give her any answers. She shut the pantry door. "We have a few hours till dinner. We'll just have to believe God will get us some food between now and then." She started to walk away.

"What if he doesn't?"

"He will," she called back. "He always has." And if he didn't, then each guest was going to dine on a few slices of syrupy orange and a single pizza bite. On her way up the stairs, she texted Galen. "Don't get up, but we're completely out of food. Any ideas for supper? You want me to call the grocery store and ask for help?"

He immediately answered: "There's a gift certificate for the pizza place in my desk drawer."

She snickered. "What have you been saving that for?"

"For now, apparently. Don't get too excited. It'll probably only buy four cheese pizzas."

Relieved, she went into Galen's office to retrieve the gift certificate, which was right where he'd said it would be. Then she went back to her desk to sort the church's mail, which was sparse: a political pamphlet; a flyer from the local furniture store; Harry's cell phone bill; and an envelope with a handwritten address and nothing in the upper left corner. She ripped into the envelope and pulled out a letter and a check for $899, made out to Open Door Church. Her first thought: what a peculiar amount. Her second thought: maybe we don't need to burn up our emergency pizza certificate after all. She turned her attention to the letter.

Dear Pastor G and Church,

You probably don't remember me, but I stayed with you for a short time many years ago. Little Daniel may remember me, though he's probably not so little anymore. He healed my bad back with one of his little prayers. I've never stopped praying for him since. Anyway, God has been good to me, and I've felt his nudging to send you this gift. I know you will put it to good use. Thank you for all you do, and please say hi to Daniel, if you're still in touch.

In Christ,
Silvia Marandola

Maggie read the letter again. She didn't remember a Silvia, but that didn't mean anything. A lot of people had come and gone through their doors over the years, and if Silvia hadn't stayed long and hadn't caused any trouble, there was a good chance Maggie wouldn't remember her. Maggie's eyes watered as she reread the part about Daniel. She missed the little guy and his mom. She'd tried to keep in touch, but Harmony never returned her calls or texts. She said a silent prayer for Daniel and then grabbed her phone so she could deposit the check.

She hesitated. There was something about that amount. $899. Yes, it was an odd amount to gift someone—why not just $900—but it was more than that. The number seemed familiar, but she didn't know why. She snapped a photo of it and put it in the account, shaking her head when she saw the church's balance, and then went to share the good news with Galen.

The number continued to niggle at her mind. Galen was upright on the couch, looking much healthier, reading his Bible. "Feeling better?" She had the urge to go to him and give him a kiss, but she didn't. It felt awkward.

"Yes, much." He looked around the room. "I'd forgotten how nice quiet can be."

"It is quiet in here. Where are the boys?" She picked the tent flyer up from the chair cushion and sat.

"Isaiah is at Jake's house, and Elijah's upstairs. He came down for a while, but then he wandered back up."

"Well I'll go roust him. He needs to go outside and get some fresh—" She stopped talking as she looked down at the flyer in her hand. "Oh Mylanta!"

Galen guffawed. "You channeling your inner Gertrude?" he quipped, lovingly poking fun at one of their former members who loved to refer to the antacid whenever something surprised her.

"No, look!" She shoved the letter and check toward him, her hand trembling.

"What is it?"

"Just read it." Her heart was pounding.

He quickly read the letter. "Wow, that's awesome! We can certainly use the funds!"

"Yes, we can." A voice in her head piped up, telling her that if he wasn't going to connect the dots, then she shouldn't do it for him, but she quickly overrode it. She held up the flyer. "Galen, look. The check is for the oddball amount of $899. This stupid tent of yours is on special. Buy one day, get one day free, for *eight ninety-nine*."

Chapter 15

Daniel

Martin was drunk again. Daniel leaned against his bedroom door, wishing it had a lock, wishing it were soundproof.

"You really expect me to believe you don't talk to other women when you're there?" his mother screeched.

"I'll talk to whoever I want wherever I want!" he slurred back.

"Not while I'm paying for your drinks!"

That's right, Mom. You tell him. Now, kick. him. out.

Martin swore. "Throw that in my face again, why don't you? You know how hard it is to find a job. You know I been looking!"

This was not true.

"I know it's hard to find a job that won't make you work. You want someone to pay you to sit around and do nothing! I'm sick of paying all the—"

Martin cut her off with a torrent of cursing and name calling, finishing with, "Do you want me to leave? Is that what you want? 'Cause I'll leave!"

Yes, Mom, that's exactly what you want. We'll be okay, just the two of us—

A loud sob told him she wasn't going to say anything of the sort. "Of *course* I don't want you to leave! I love you! I just don't want to come home from work and find you've spent all day drinking at the bar, using my money to buy other women drinks!"

More cursing from Martin. Daniel couldn't take it anymore. He ripped open his bedroom door and headed for the exit, not surprised to see a half-empty whiskey bottle lazily dangling from Martin's hand.

"Where do you think you're going?" his mother said to his back.

"Out." He reached for the knob.

"No, you're not! It's a school night!"

He laughed bitterly and turned toward her. "I love it when you pretend to be a real mother and worry about things like a good night's sleep."

Martin came at him. "Don't you talk to your mother like that!"

Daniel raised his chin. "Really? You're going to tell me how to talk to my mother?"

Martin was still coming, and Daniel raised his voice. "You are nothing but a piece of—"

The whiskey bottle shattered on the wall beside Daniel's head, spraying him with booze and glass shards. He jerked his face away and brought his hand to his cheek, checking for cuts, for blood. It didn't hurt, but his eyes filled with tears anyway. He kept his face turned to hide his tears and said, "I really hate you, Harmony." Then he opened the door and walked out. He slammed the door shut and hurried away, knowing Martin would follow him, but also knowing that he wouldn't follow him far. He was too lazy.

He ran outside and into the alley, where he stopped and leaned against the cool brick wall to gather himself. He wiped at his cheek and hair, disgusted by the stench of whiskey. When he pulled his sleeve away, there was a small streak of pink blood on his cuff. Great. So he probably had glass splinters in his face. Just what he needed. He waited till his tears were dry and then he texted Ember: "You up?"

It took her several minutes to answer, but she was awake.

"I'm outside," he wrote. "Wanna hang?"

She didn't answer, and he had almost given up on her when she appeared at the end of the alley, looking as beautiful as he'd ever seen her. She'd dyed her hair again, and it was bright pink in the streetlights. She had a hot pink backpack on, and it looked stuffed to the brink. "You running away?" he said, trying to be funny.

She started toward him, and he wanted to go to her, to wrap his arms around her, but he stayed where he was, leaning against the wall, with one sole pressed against the bricks and his hands in his pockets, trying to play it cool.

Her brows drew together. "You're bleeding."

"Yeah. Martin decided my face needed a whiskey bottle imprint."

She reeled back. "He hit you?"

"No, he just threw it at the wall. He doesn't have the guts to hit me."

She reached up and touched his cheek, and a thrill shot through his body. "You've got glass. Let me get it." She took off the backpack and put it between her feet. Then she went to work on his face with both hands, gently. "Only two pieces that I can see. There. I got one of them out." She flicked something too small to see behind her.

"I guess I should be thankful. At least this one doesn't hit my mom. He just mooches off her, cheats on her, and calls her names." He didn't want to talk about it anymore. "What's in the bag?"

She snapped her gum. "Goodies. Vodka, Mountain Dew, and bud."

Revival

He hated vodka and pot. He liked Mountain Dew, though. "Good on all three counts."

Chapter 16

Galen

Galen threw all his energy into planning the revival. He didn't have a lot of time because his tent coupon had an expiration date. And even if it hadn't, Maine summers did. He didn't want to be shoveling snow out of his revival tent.

Pastor Udi had advised Galen to pick a site separate from Open Door, so attendees wouldn't immediately associate the event with the shelter. At first, Galen had bristled at this advice, but then he'd accepted it. He asked a few churches in town, ones with large properties, but neither were excited about helping him, even when he offered a joint venture. He didn't let them dampen his enthusiasm, though, and called the town office to ask about the town park. This was met with a resounding no. He called the town rec department. What about one of their baseball fields? No. He called the local car dealership, which was owned by a Christian family: no. He called a few farmers with big fields: no. WaterWoopPark water park: no. He sat back in his chair and stared at the wall. Realizing that he probably should've prayed for a spot before he started calling around, he bowed his head and requested heavenly help.

His growling stomach was the only response he got.

He was on his way to the kitchen when he ran into Odin, who was on his way to the door with a giant canvas backpack slung over his shoulder. "Moving out?" Galen asked jovially.

"Yes, finally."

"Congratulations. You have someplace safe to go?"

"Yeah," Odin said as if Galen were a moron. "I got a bus ticket to Manchester."

Galen couldn't imagine what was waiting for him in Manchester, but he didn't ask. "Awesome." He gave his backpack a friendly pat. "You take care." He turned to head downstairs for a snack.

"Can you give me a ride to the bus station?"

Galen suppressed a groan. "Sure can. Give me just a sec."

"The bus leaves in like ten minutes."

Of course it did. "All right, let's go." Abandoning his snack quest, he followed Odin out through the front door and to his truck, where the keys were in the ignition. The chances of anyone stealing his truck were slim to none.

Odin complained about the worship music, but Galen didn't touch the volume button. "Just be thankful I'm not singing along." They drove the rest of the way sans conversation, with Galen scanning both sides of the road for a good revival spot.

And then he saw it. Curl Up and Dye. The town's premiere beauty salon. He didn't know anyone who could afford to get a haircut there, let alone any of the fancier things they offered. But the owner was a believer, who more than once had donated supplies to Maggie's little church salon for the homeless. He had complete confidence she would love to have a giant tent staked down in the field behind her upscale salon.

He didn't even put the truck in park at the bus station, but did resist the urge to push Odin out through the door. Odin didn't thank him, of course, but this was okay because Galen had bigger things on his mind. He tried to obey the speed limits on his way back to the salon, mostly succeeding, and then pulled his old, clunky truck in between a sleek red convertible and a loaded Cadillac SUV.

An electronic bell chimed as he entered, and as he waited for his eyes to adjust to the dim lights, he realized that he was going to feel pretty goofy if Phyllis wasn't there.

But she was. "Well, hello, Pastor G!" she cooed. "Stepping out on your wife?"

He laughed and approached the counter. "No. Only one woman for this mess." He ran a hand through his thinning hair. "I've stopped in because I've got an odd question for you."

"I'm ready."

But was she, really? He took a deep breath. "I think God wants me to hold an old-fashioned tent revival, and I was wondering if we could use the field behind your salon?"

She didn't even hesitate. "Of course!"

"And your parking lot."

"Absolutely."

The fake bell chimed again, and Phyllis forgot about Galen for a minute as she welcomed an exceptionally tanned woman and showed her to her masseuse's room. Then she came back to the counter. "When is your shindig?"

He didn't know, had been waiting for a location before picking a date. "How does two weeks from now sound?"

She raised her perfectly penciled eyebrows. "Two weeks? You must have everything else pulled together, then?"

He did not. "Two weeks. Saturday and Sunday. We'll be out of your hair by Sunday night." He wondered what he'd do if the field was full of people hungry for the Gospel. Would he really call a halt to the whole thing because his tent coupon was only good for two days?

"You okay?"

He chuckled and rubbed his jaw. "Yeah, just thinking about lots of moving parts."

"I would imagine! Who have you got coming to speak at this thing?"

Galen hesitated. She was assuming he wasn't qualified. She was correct. But he didn't have anyone else. "As of right now, me. But maybe God will send someone else. That would be fine too."

She smiled. "And the music? You've got some bands lined up?"

He thought of Harry and the smile fell off his face. "Not yet, no. I needed to firm up the location first."

"Oh! Well, my nephew has a band!"

Oh dear.

"They're fantastic. A good little local Christian rock band. I'm sure they'd love to play for you!"

Was this a quid pro quo situation? Was he going to lose his field if he said no to this?

"They call themselves Blanktified!"

He tried to hide his horror, but she saw it.

"You know, like a combination of blood and sanctified ... Blanktified! Catchy, right?"

Chapter 17

Maggie

Maggie wanted to find the Udis and ring their necks. Galen had suffered a major heart attack because he was overworked and overstressed and their solution was that Galen should plan a major event to recruit new help. But were they going to help with this event? True, they had offered to pay for the tent, but their charity had ended there. Galen had asked, begged even, Steven to speak, but he was conveniently busy that weekend, and Galen had asked them to help him plan and market the event, but they said they didn't have time to do it in the next two weeks.

And so, Galen had undertaken a giant project, by himself, again. She did as much as she could to help. She tried to keep the shelter running as he looked for more bands, more preachers, and more folding chairs. He had some teen band coming, but Maggie hadn't laid eyes on them yet, and wasn't confident they even existed. All she knew was that they didn't have enough equipment, so now Galen was trying to beg for and borrow extra microphones, amps, and speakers.

Every morning, he got up before the sun came up to go walk the property and pray, and he came home late at night, when she was too exhausted for conversation. He never saw his boys. He never saw her. She told herself that things would calm down after the revival, but she knew this wasn't true. She tried to feed him fruits and vegetables, but she still had nightly nightmares of him dying. Frequently, she'd roll over and put her hand on his chest just to make sure he was still alive.

When she saw the stack of five hundred printed out flyers, she almost had a heart attack of her own. She couldn't believe how amateur they looked. True, Galen wasn't a graphic designer, but these were ridiculous.

TENT REVIVAL!
July 28 & 29!
Dynamic speaking, prayer, and music!
Featuring Galen Turney, Blanktified, and Harry Orthweiler!
Don't Miss Worship Under the Tent!
Curl Up and Dye
99 Main Street, Mattawooptock

Maggie couldn't understand Galen's decisions regarding capitalization and was worried that someone would think they were featuring some kind of performer named Miss Worship.

And he hadn't even included the times. Was Galen planning to talk all day for two days? How could he have worked so hard, invested so much time, and still have such a terrible plan?

"Honey, I don't think we should hang these," she said tentatively, not wanting to sound critical.

"Why not?" He set his coffee cup down on her desk in the church office.

How should she begin? Should she ask him where he got the kindergarten clip art? "For starters, we forgot the time." She watched that register. He couldn't argue with that one. "And I wonder if, instead of naming the artists, who no one has ever heard of, not to mention that the band's name is ridiculous, I wonder if we should just say 'featuring local musicians'?"

He nodded slowly as he stared at the stack of flyers. "Yeah, that's a good idea. But we've already paid to have these printed." He looked up at her. "I wish you'd said something before."

She suppressed a groan. She would have, if he'd consulted her. "Please, don't hang these. I'll make an electronic version, include all the times, and then blast it all over social media. We don't need physical flyers."

His face twisted up in horror. "Of course we need flyers! Not everybody is on social media!"

"Yes, they are. Okay, I'll print like ten flyers, once I have the new version done."

He thought about it and then nodded. "Fine."

"Fine. And, have you called any other churches and asked for more worship teams?"

The muscles in his jaw bulged. "Of *course* I did."

"You mind if I give it a shot?"

"I already called everybody, and they all said no, so you calling them is going to amount to harassment. They're not going to change their minds just because we badger them!"

She didn't appreciate his volume. "You called every single church within fifty miles?" she said as quietly as possible.

"Yes, I did."

"Fine." She turned away from him and went to her computer to make a new flyer, and as she typed, she realized how much she was growing to hate the word *revival.*

Ten minutes later, Galen stuck his head out of his office, looking excited. "Please add Kevin McLaughlin to the flyer. He's going to speak."

Maggie tried to look excited. "I didn't know you invited him!"

"I didn't! He heard about it and emailed me, offering to help."

"Great!" She forced a smile, and Galen went back into his office. Kevin McLaughlin was a local retired missionary who had served in Africa for thirty years. He was a wonderful man. He was also ancient.

As she added his name to her advertisement, she was near tears. Her church was running on fumes and she feared it was going to run out of gas very publicly, under a large tent behind Curl Up and Dye.

Chapter 18

Galen

It was time. July 28. Five a.m. Galen swung his feet onto the floor.

He'd hardly slept a wink. Not because he was worried. He wasn't. He was excited. He was certain God was going to do something. He knew this wasn't going to be as big and grand as other churches' events, but he was used to that. Open Door projects were always done on a shoestring with a skeleton crew.

He got up before his alarm went off, hurriedly read his Scripture for the day, and then went to walk around the property, as he had almost every morning for eight years. He'd missed a few mornings due to sickness and injuries, including an entire week with a sprained knee sustained from falling off the church roof. But despite those missed laps, he'd worn a groove around the church, and he walked the path now with his hands in the air, asking God to bring the right people, to give him the right words to say, to give them open ears and open hearts. He asked that people might feel God's love and receive salvation and that Blanktified wouldn't be as bad as he feared. He'd invited them to rehearse, but they hadn't been able to because their lead singer couldn't get out of his shift at WaterWoopPark, which was in its peak season. They'd assured him that they didn't need to practice and would show up when he needed them. He asked that God would protect everyone as they traveled to and from the meeting and that Harry would be in a good mood for his music sets. And then he said, "Amen." He stopped and looked at the church, silently thanking God for it. How he loved this place, the land itself, the building, all the people who had come and gone and were there now. His heart was near to bursting with affection for all of it, and he just knew that today was going to be a game-changer for their ministry.

He went back into the parsonage to wake his sons, so they could help him load the chairs. It would take him a few trips to get them all to Curl Up and Dye in his pickup. Isaiah groaned and complained, but Elijah was excited, to Galen's delight.

"How many people do you think will come?" Elijah asked.

"I don't know, bud. We've got about a hundred chairs, but if more people come, there'll be plenty of room to stand."

"Wow, a hundred people!" Elijah said, wide-eyed. "We've never had that many people in church before!"

Dan used to, Galen thought.

"You do know that Blanktified is terrible," Isaiah grumbled.

Galen looked at him. "And you didn't think to mention this before?"

Isaiah shrugged and walked away.

"Hey, have you actually heard them play?"

Isaiah grabbed two chairs and headed back toward Galen and the truck. "No, but I know who they are, and they're total dorks."

"So, for all you know, they could be totally talented dorks."

Isaiah gave him a dubious look and handed the chairs up to his brother.

With a bed full of metal chairs, Galen and his boys drove across town to the fancy salon. The folks from The Tent Shop were already setting up, and Galen breathed a sigh of relief at the sight of them. He hadn't been worried about them showing up, but he was still mightily glad to see the whites of their eyes. He strode across the dewy grass and shook their hands, leaving the wrestling with the chairs to his boys, who soon complained, and Galen hustled back to the truck to help.

By the time they delivered their second truckload, the tent was upright, and it looked a lot smaller than Galen had envisioned. "That's the thousand-foot tent?" he asked the men.

It was clear this wasn't the first time they'd been asked that question. "Yes sir," one of them said, "one thousand square feet."

Galen wasn't sure they'd be able to get a hundred chairs under it, but he also wasn't worried. He didn't know if a hundred people were going to show up; they could start with seventy chairs and see what happened.

As Galen had requested, The Tent Shop set up a small stage at the front of the tent. He went to it and began to set up the microphones and speakers, feeling lighter than he had in years.

Chapter 19

Galen

Nine o'clock. The Tent Shop workers had left. Galen's boys sat in the front row while he stood on the corner of the small platform up front with his arms folded across his chest. They were the only three people on the property.

Curl Up and Dye hadn't opened yet, so Galen's truck was the only one in the parking lot. Blanktified was supposed to open with a worship set, but they weren't there yet. For this, Galen was grateful. He was embarrassed that no one was there to listen.

He couldn't look at his boys, didn't want to deal with Elijah's confusion, or worse, with Isaiah's I-told-you-so. He sat down on the edge of the stage, which was so close to the grass that his knees pointed toward the tent ceiling at a painfully sharp angle. He didn't know if he'd ever get back up again.

"I don't think anyone's coming," Isaiah said. The lack of criticism in his tone touched Galen's heart.

"It's early," Galen said. "Maybe people are planning to come later. Maybe I started too early."

"No matter what happens," Isaiah said, "it's not your fault, Dad. You've done a good job. People around here just aren't into Jesus."

Gravel crunched in the parking lot and all three of them looked up, even though they couldn't see anything except the giant salon. With effort, Galen got himself back to a standing position and left the tent to see if Blanktified was finally on the scene. Galen saw two cars and for a second, got excited, thinking that Blanktified had brought friends, but then two teenagers spilled out of each car and he realized it was just four band members and three guitars. Their lackadaisical attitude suggested either they didn't know they were late or didn't care.

"Good morning!" Galen called out. "Do you need help with anything?"

"I think we're all set," the tallest of them said. He shook long black bangs out of his eyes. "Just show us where to set up."

"Right this way." Galen turned back toward the tent, his stomach tight. What had he done? This was a disaster. No, that wasn't quite true. To be a disaster, something had to occur. This was a nonoccurrence. This was an empty tent in a field and six teenagers.

The tall kid stepped up onto the stage and turned toward the empty chairs. "This is cool," he said, sounded completely sincere.

The sole female member of the band nodded in agreement. "Yeah, this is going to be our best gig ever."

Had they had another gig before? Galen was skeptical.

It took them fifteen minutes to plug in all their cords, set up their drums, tune their guitars, and do their sound checks. Then they looked at Galen. "You want us to start?" the tall kid said. He was apparently also the lead singer because he was standing in the middle. "Or do you want us to wait for someone to get here?"

"Go ahead and start. Maybe the music will draw people in." Galen didn't think this would be the case, but it was worth a shot. "But first, introduce yourselves," he said because he still didn't know their names.

"The mop-haired gangly kid gave him a toothy smile and then spoke into the microphone, "Good morning and welcome to Mattawooptock's first annual tent revival."

Where had he gotten that idea? This certainly wasn't going to be an annual affair.

"My name is Todd Daley, and to my right is my little sis, Alexandra Daley."

Alexandra wasn't so little. She was almost as tall as Todd and must have stood at least six feet.

"Behind me on the drums is Jake Cooley and to my left is David Meek. And together we are Blanktified!" The kid was a showman. Galen had to give them that. He gave a loud introductory strum on his electric guitar and Galen's cheeks vibrated. Then Todd Daley opened his mouth and screamed into the microphone as two more guitars joined the discordant rumpus and the drummer began to bang on the drums with a time signature that seemed to go from 4/4 to 6/8 and back again all within a single measure.

It sounded exactly like one might expect an unskilled, unpracticed teenage garage band to sound, and Galen wondered how he had expected anything else. He looked around: the empty tent; the cloudy sky; the four headbangers; his two sons. How *had* he expected anything else? Because he'd just believed what he wanted to believe. And he'd been so terribly wrong.

Isaiah's eyes caught his, and what he saw there made him wish for some I-told-you-so.

Revival

His oldest son was looking at him with pity.

Chapter 20

Galen

At a quarter to ten, Blanktified finished their opening set, and Elijah clapped for them, which spurred Galen to applaud as well. "Thanks, guys," he forced out.

Lead singer and guitarist Todd nodded gratefully, obviously pleased with a job well done. "Now what do you want us to do?" he asked, looking out at the empty chairs.

Galen hesitated. His plan had been to start speaking, but there was no one to speak to. "You guys can play another set this afternoon, if you want, but you don't have to hang around till then. You can leave your stuff. I'll be here, and nothing will happen to it."

They looked disappointed.

"Or you can stay if you want to."

They silently consulted one another, making no move to leave. Apparently, they wanted to stay.

Galen looked at his boys. "Want me to call your mom to come pick you up?"

"I want to stay," Elijah said quickly, and Isaiah nodded his agreement.

"Someone's here," Jake the drummer said, staring at the back of the salon.

"Might be our mom," Alexandra said. "She was supposed to be here when we started."

Todd gave Galen an apologetic smile. "She's always late."

"No worries," Galen said quickly. He tried to be patient as he waited to see who would come walking around the building, and when no one came, he worried that the vehicle they'd heard was a salon customer. He couldn't stand the suspense, so he left the tent to investigate, and met ex-missionary Kevin McLaughlin as he was coming around the corner. He stopped and leaned on his shiny wooden cane. Oh, it was that time already. Why had he scheduled him to speak so early? Galen's embarrassment deepened. "Thanks so much for coming," he called out, offering his hand.

Kevin took it, looking back over his shoulder at the almost empty parking lot. "I guess I'm one of the few?"

Galen's shoulders sagged. A weird calm overtook him. Standing here in front of this man of God stripped him of pretense, and he had no desire to pretend anything. "Yes. You're one of the few. I'm so sorry, I may have gotten you out here for nothing. We've got the teenage band here, but I'm afraid no one else is going to show up."

Kevin slapped a hand on Galen's shoulder with a strength that surprised him. "Don't be foolish, son. It's never for nothing. God's Word will not return void. Let's go talk to the teen band." He stepped around Galen and headed up the small slope of lawn, toward the tent, and Galen had to hustle to keep up with him.

Kevin stepped under the tent just as the rain started to fall.

Galen looked up at the sky. *Seriously, God? What are you trying to do to me?*

The senior servant walked right up to Alexandra and stuck his hand out. "Good morning, young lady. My name is Kevin McLaughlin. What's yours?"

Her black lipsticked lips widened in a sincere smile. "Alexandra. I've heard you speak before. You came to my church."

Kevin nodded. "Yes, I think I've spoken at every church within a hundred miles, asking for prayer and money." He chuckled and went on to shake the next teen's hand. Then he thanked them for volunteering their talents on this fine rainy day.

Galen wondered if he'd still be using the word *talent* once he'd heard them play. Galen settled into an aisle seat as the rain picked up, the sound of it on the tent top both frustrating and beautiful—a fitting soundtrack for the last several years of Galen's life.

Kevin stepped up to the microphone, but then looked over Galen's head toward the back of the tent. "Well, I was going to start talking, but looks like we've got a few new guests, Pastor G, if you'd like to go greet them."

Incredulous, Galen turned to see a senior couple had entered their tent. They wore raincoats, and thick drops of water fell from the brim of the woman's hat. He jumped up and headed their way, forcing himself to dampen his enthusiasm so as not to scare them off. "Welcome," he said, offering his hand, which the gentleman took. "I'm Galen Turney."

"Howard Jackson, and this is my wife, Ruby."

"Pleasure to meet you both." Galen shook her hand too, and she seemed surprised. "Would you like to have a seat?"

They didn't seem at ease, exactly, but they also weren't running away, and Galen tried to relax. He wished he'd done more research. Had all those famous revivals started small and slow? He looked at Kevin, expecting him to start speaking, but instead, Kevin looked at Galen, nodded toward the newcomers, who were focused on settling into their second row seats and not yet looking at him, and came down off the platform. Galen sensed that Kevin wanted him to join him, so he did.

By the time Galen got to them, Kevin was sitting in front of them and had already introduced himself. "Where are you folks from?"

The teenagers grew bored and started to chat amongst themselves, and Galen was glad to see his sons involved in the conversation.

"Up in Rangeley, originally," Howard said, taking off his raincoat. "But we recently moved here to be closer to our grandkids. We've been looking for a church to call home, but nothing's clicked yet."

Of course, they hadn't tried the local homeless shelter yet. Why would they? Galen sat down in a front row chair, turning to face the conversation.

"I understand," Kevin said.

"So you're not the pastor here?" Howard asked Kevin.

Kevin pointed at Galen. "No, sir. He is."

Galen smiled. "I pastor at Open Door Church, over on—"

"Isn't that the one with the homeless shelter?" Ruby exclaimed, not even trying to keep the horror out of her voice.

Chapter 21

Galen

Harry was in a good mood, and he was doing a bang up job of playing a worship set. Howard and Ruby were stoically singing along on one side of the aisle, while Blanktified sang along on the other with their hands in the air. Isaiah and Elijah stood behind Blanktified, looking bored. They weren't Harry's biggest fans.

Kevin took Galen by the arm and tugged him toward the back of the tent. "That's your gifting, son."

What? How could he look at any part of this and think of the word *gifting*?

Kevin read his mind. "Talking to them, like you did. You might not be a lights-and-smoke-up-front kind of pastor, but you've got the one-on-one thing down pat!" He patted him on the back for emphasis.

"Thank you," Galen managed.

"You're welcome. Now, I'm starving. I'm going to go find some food. What can I get you?"

Galen wanted to kick himself. Why hadn't he brought food for his guest speakers and musicians? He didn't even have any water to offer them, unless one counted what was falling out of the sky.

"No, thank you."

"Nonsense. You've got to eat. Tell me what to get you, or I'll surprise you, and you might not like it."

Galen grinned. "No, really. You don't have to get me anything. I'll be fine."

"Pickled eggs it is!" Kevin laughed, spun on his cane, and headed out into the rain. Someone from away might have assumed he was joking, but Galen knew the local pizza place had pickled eggs flying out the door, so he thought maybe he was about to get just what he'd been promised, and hoped that Kevin also brought him some Saltines to go with them.

Harry was finishing up, Galen could tell, so he headed for the front to finally give the first short sermon he'd prepared for the time slot. "Welcome, again, to each of you. I know we're not a big crowd, but I am grateful for each of you, and I'd like to share a testimony with you. I'd like to tell you about how God showed me he wanted me to be a pastor. Now, this is kind of a crazy story, but it is one hundred percent true, so I challenge you to take me at my word and let this example of God's power suggest to you just what God is capable of ..."

Howard's face was impassive. Ruby looked skeptical. The members of Blanktified looked riveted. They were locals and may have heard the story. Galen told it often, and rumors about it abounded. Those locals who didn't believe that Galen had been shot dead and resurrected made a sport of coming up with alternative explanations to what the witnesses had seen.

As Galen continued, Howard grew more involved in the story and Ruby's face softened. "I am not a gifted speaker, and it's difficult to put this story into words, to explain what I saw, how I felt. No matter how many times I tell the story, it falls short of the reality I went through that day, but I'm not sure God wants me to be able to explain it exactly because it will be a surprise for you when you get there. No matter what you are picturing in your minds right now, the real deal is so much stronger, and you're going to love it. And I don't want anyone to miss out on it. I died, and I met Jesus, and it was beyond awesome. Each of you is going to die too, and I want you to meet Jesus. But there's only one way to do that, and that is to ask him for that gift." He was fairly confident that everyone under the tent already knew Jesus, but he continued with his plan, just in case.

His voice softened as he chose his words carefully. He'd now shared the Gospel thousands of times, and it still hadn't become rote. "Each one of us has done something wrong in our lives. We've hurt someone, or we've hurt ourselves. The Bible calls that sin. God is pure good, so he can have nothing to do with sin. Sin separates us from God. It puts up a wall we can't get over, around, or tear down. It blocks us from access to him. But Jesus paid a penalty that tore down that wall. He sacrificed himself. He gave his life, and that sacrifice washed away the bad thing you did. All the bad things you did. He did this because he loves you, because he wants you to have access to God, because he doesn't want you to have to live on the other side of that wall. But you have to receive this gift of his. You have to ask him to forgive you for those sins, and you have to let his love into your life.

"God doesn't force himself on anyone. He wants you, but he wants you to want him back, and he'll wait for you to ask." Galen took a big breath. "All it takes is a sorry heart and a simple prayer. You have to truly be sorry for your sin, and then you have to ask God to take it away, and he will. So, I'm asking you right now. Are you sorry for putting up that wall between yourself and God? Do you want it torn down? Do you want direct access to the God of the universe, to the source of all that is good, to the source of real love? If your answer is yes, please say this prayer with me. You can say it out loud, or you can say it silently in your heart. God will hear it either way."

Galen bowed his head and squeezed his eyes shut. As he prayed the familiar prayer aloud, he prayed another prayer beneath it: *If there is anyone who doesn't know you, touch their heart. Bring them to you right now.* "Jesus, thank you for sacrificing yourself for me. I know I don't deserve that kind of love. I am sorry for my sins. I am sorry for doing selfish things that hurt people, that hurt you. Please forgive me of my sins and set me free of them. Set me free of the ways of this world. Please tear down the wall between me and God. I want you in my life. I want to follow you, starting right now. In your name, I pray. Amen."

When he looked up, Howard was putting on his coat. Galen's heart sank. "I'm going to ask Blanktified to come sing a *worship* song for you now." He emphasized the word *worship* as best he could. He knew that, with the right heart attitude, any song could be a worship song, but he really didn't want them to sing another song about slaying their inner dragons with spirit swords. "If you prayed that prayer today, please come talk to me soon. I'd love to help you get to know Jesus better. I'd love to help you in general." He nodded toward Todd, and he stepped down off the platform.

Howard stood and helped Ruby with her coat. She was having trouble getting it on; it looked like she was dealing with some back pain. Galen tried not to pounce on them, but stayed close enough that they could easily speak to him if they wanted to.

Apparently, Howard did. He grabbed Galen's hand and pumped it up and down. "That was quite a story you just told."

"Yes, sir—"

"We're going to get going."

Ruby was already walking away, slowly, favoring her right side.

"My wife's caught a chill, so we're going to go get warmed up. But you've given us a lot to think about, and I thank you." He sucked his lips in. "I'd like to say we'll be back tomorrow, and we may be, but what time's your normal service, at the church?"

Knock me over with a feather. "Ten o'clock."

"Great! We'll probably see you there." He stepped out into the aisle. "And we'll be praying for the continued success of your little tent meeting here." He smiled, nodded, and then headed for his wife, who was waiting at the edge of the tent.

Galen watched them go, speechless, as Todd Daley of Blanktified played an exceptionally loud G7 while his sister played a B flat. It was a powerful sound.

Chapter 22

Maggie

Maggie was braiding an eight-year-old's hair in the church salon when her husband and sons appeared in the doorway. "Hey, guys! How's it going?"

Elijah collapsed onto the worn couch. "Dad made us leave."

She raised an eyebrow. "Oh yeah? So you were having fun?"

Isaiah sat beside his brother in a less dramatic fashion. "Not *fun*, exactly, but it was pretty cool."

She was so encouraged to hear this. She'd been worried that the three of them had been sitting there alone in the rain. "How'd you get away?" she asked Galen as she snapped a hair tie onto the end of the braid. "You're all set, kiddo." She unsnapped the plastic sheet from the girl's neck and whisked it off her. Her still-wet trimmings fell to the floor.

"Kevin is supervising Blanktified, and when we left, they were the only people there."

Uh-oh. She opened her mouth, but no words came out.

"We did have a few people," Galen hurried to say, defensively, "but they left."

"That's okay," she said slowly, a little peeved that he was being defensive with her. She wasn't being critical. "Do you have time for some lunch, then?"

"Yes! I'm starving!" Elijah said, standing up.

"I wasn't talking to you, but, yes, I'll feed you too." She looked at her husband.

"No, thank you. I want to get back, and Kevin bought me an Italian."

"And a Coke! And Dad drank it!"

Galen scowled at his youngest son. "Tattletale."

"The doctor said you're not supposed to have soda!" Elijah said.

"He said no caffeine," Galen corrected.

Maggie didn't bother to remind him that Coke was well caffeinated.

"Anyway, I want to get back because I'm not confident Kevin is enjoying the Blanktified show."

"Why?" Isaiah asked. Now he was the one being defensive.

It must run in the blood, she thought.

"They're pretty good," Isaiah said.

Galen's expression suggested he disagreed.

"Isn't Harry there?" she asked.

"No, he played his set and then left."

"How? I dropped him off, but I didn't go pick him up."

"No idea."

She could tell he was about to leave again and she didn't want him to. "So, it's going well, then?"

He hesitated and then shrugged. "Not really. It's raining, and only two people showed up."

"Oh, I'm sorry. Well, it's still early. And maybe, if Harry ever shows back up here, I can leave him in charge of the shelter, and the boys and I can come back and fill some chairs."

"Yeah!" Elijah said.

"Don't bother," Galen said quickly. "Stay here where it's dry and quiet." He stepped back. "I've got to go." He turned away. "Love you," he said, without looking at her.

"Love you too," she said to the empty hallway. She looked at Isaiah. "Was it really that bad?"

He was looking at his phone. "Yeah, it was pretty bad."

"No, it wasn't!" Elijah chirped. "There just aren't many people there because it's raining."

Maggie let out a long breath. "Why don't you guys go over to the parsonage. Isaiah, would you please get some water boiling for some mac and cheese? I've got to finish up Brenda's hair." The little girl's mom had just leaned back into Maggie's sink. "But I'll be home after that."

Isaiah groaned as if she'd asked him to shovel lead.

"Or, if you don't want to eat, that's fine too."

"I can boil water!" Elijah said. "I'm not a little kid!"

"You're right. You take over the boiling water. Thank you."

The boys disappeared. "Is G okay?" Brenda asked.

Maggie had no idea. "I think so."

"He seemed kind of grumpy. Maybe after haircuts, we can go check out this tent thing. Might be fun."

"I agree. I plan to go check it out too." As Maggie massaged the soap into Brenda's hair, her mind was a few miles away, under a big rental tent. She tried to picture it, and the image pained her chest. How her husband must hate the sight of all those empty chairs. *God,* she silently prayed, *there's got to be someone nearby who needs what we're offering. Please bring them to us. And whether this is a success or a flop, please bring my husband through it in good health. Please don't let him get stressed out about this.* She began to rinse out the shampoo. *And also, God, I pray for my marriage. I don't even know what's wrong with us, but please fix it.*

"Um, Maggie?"

She looked down at Brenda. "Yeah?"

"That water is *really* cold."

"Oh sorry!" Maggie hurried to turn the knob marked with the little red circle.

Chapter 23

Daniel

It was ninety-five degrees out with humidity that felt like a steam room. Martin had friends over, so Daniel had left the apartment. He didn't want to be there anyway. They didn't have air conditioning. He wondered what Ember was doing, but he didn't want to act like a stalker. She was probably out with her old, hairy boyfriend, and if that was the case, he definitely didn't want to text her. He didn't want to seem desperate.

She'd been increasing the distance between them lately, which he both hated and appreciated. Hated because he was in love with her. Appreciated because he didn't think they were ever going to be together and he didn't like it when she teased him and got his hopes up. Hoping the ocean would bring some sort of breeze, Daniel started walking toward the Eastern Prom. He didn't pass many people on the way. It was too hot out for walking. A few people rode bikes and one lunatic was jogging, but other than that, the streets were quiet. As he grew closer to the water, he saw a peppering of tourists, but nothing like a normal weekend in July. They were still there, he knew that, but they were all holed up in their air-conditioned hotel rooms taking in their ocean views through the windows.

He reached the park and lifted his head toward the water, anticipating a breeze that wasn't quite there. Even the Atlantic was stuffy and still. He looked out toward Peaks Island, wishing he had enough for a ferry ride. It was probably cooler out there. He decided to make his own breeze and took the middle swing on an empty swing set. He bounced a little to make sure the rusted old thing would hold him and then deciding that he didn't really care if it did, he pushed off and began to pump like a little kid.

The breeze felt glorious.

He pumped until his legs burned and then he eased off and relaxed, enjoying the motion and the wind through his sticky hair. On one of his descents, he noticed an old rust bucket parked between him and the ocean. Something about it gave him pause. Did it look familiar? He had never been that into cars, couldn't really tell one make from another, but there was something about this one. He squinted, straining to see inside the car, and saw a flash of pink hair.

Pink hair doesn't always mean Ember, he told himself and yet he stuck his feet into the dirt to drag himself to a stop. Then he stood up, a little wobbly, and headed toward the car. As he drew nearer, he saw it *was* Ember in the passenger seat, and a man he didn't recognize was behind the wheel. It wasn't her ancient boyfriend. This guy was even older. Way older. Who was it? Had she moved on to a different old man? He couldn't hear them, but he could tell by their body language that they were arguing. He picked up his speed.

The man was hollering, but Daniel couldn't make out the words. Ember was pressed up against her open window, shrinking away from him. Why didn't she get out of the car? *Open the stupid door*, Daniel tried to will her to do it. As he got closer, the man's voice got louder, more threatening, and Daniel broke into a run. "Hey!" he hollered, trying to sound tough. The man looked at him, looked at Ember, and started the car. Then they were driving away. Foolishly, Daniel gave chase, hollering for them to stop, but he knew this was ridiculous. The man wasn't going to stop.

He stopped and tried to catch his breath, which wasn't easy since he felt like he was breathing water. He fumbled to get his phone out of his pocket and texted, "U OK?"

Predictably, she didn't answer.

Daniel hated going shirtless, was too self-conscious to stride around showing off his pale skin and bones, but he made an exception this time. He took his T-shirt off, tucked it into his back pocket, and then, holding his phone in his hand, headed up the hill toward home. He doubted that's where mystery creep was taking Ember, but he wanted to be there just in case it was.

Chapter 24

Galen

At six o'clock, a group of people strode through the wet grass toward the tent, and Galen's heart leapt with hope. But as Blanktified got out of their chairs to greet them, Galen realized they were the parents and families of the young musicians. This was only a small letdown. They were still people, and they sat down. Galen went over to them, introduced himself, and thanked them for their kids' service. "I am so impressed. They're talented, of course, but I'm even more impressed by their servant's hearts. They've been here most of the day, and haven't complained at all."

One of the mothers grinned. She'd said her name ten seconds ago, and Galen had already forgotten it. "This is their first gig outside of our church, so I think they're thrilled."

"How has the turnout been?" one of the fathers asked.

It occurred to Galen to lie, and he was both surprised and ashamed that he'd had the notion. "It hasn't been good, I'm afraid."

The man didn't look surprised by this. "Yeah, this is a tough town. Good for you for giving it a shot, though. We sure do need revival around here."

Galen forced a smile in response. "I know you are all here to see your kids perform, but I had Kevin McLaughlin on the schedule for right now. Of course, that schedule is flexible ..." Galen didn't really want to change it up on Kevin. He'd been such a saint, and maybe he was ready to get out of there.

"No, no, that's okay," a mother said. "We're happy to go with whatever you've got planned. They are playing again, though, right?"

He nodded quickly. "Absolutely. They're going to close out the evening." It was actually Harry on the schedule, but he was MIA. Galen had planned an altar call with Harry playing softly in the background. He didn't know if Blanktified could play softly, but he also didn't think he'd need to give an altar call. He thanked the parents and went to the front of the tent to introduce Kevin.

"I'm so grateful to have Kevin McLaughlin here with us today. He's been a huge support to me today, both physically and spiritually. Kevin is a man after God's own heart if I've ever known one. He served as a missionary in West Africa for more than twenty years, and he has so many stories to tell. I'm excited that you're here to hear from him, and I pray his experiences bless you in many ways." He swung a hand toward Kevin. "Ladies and gentlemen, Kevin McLaughlin."

Pushing up on his cane, Kevin came to a shaky stand. The day had taken its toll on him. Probably too many trips across the uneven wet grass. Galen gave him a hand with the small step up onto the stage and then went to take a seat in the front row.

As Kevin reached the adjustable music stand that was serving as their podium, Galen felt a breeze on his cheek and smelled lavender. He turned to see his wife sliding into the seat beside him, and the sight of her made him feel lighter. "Did Harry come back to the church?"

She shook her head and leaned in toward him. "I left Isaiah in charge." She showed him the phone in her hand. "He'll text if anyone new shows up or anything goes wrong."

This was a new one. Isaiah was fifteen, and leaving him in charge of a homeless shelter was a tall order. Galen was proud that his son was mature enough to take on the task, alarmed that he was doing so, and shocked that he would agree to it.

He admired his wife for a few more seconds and then turned his attention to Kevin, who was already well into his message.

"They didn't believe me! And that's okay!" He was quite animated for someone his age, Galen thought, someone who had endured the day he had. This was the third message he'd shared. "You don't have to believe me either, if you don't want to. It's not my job to make you believe me. It's just my job to share my testimony. I'll leave the believing part up to you and the Holy Spirit! So, I get this call to go to the next village, a place by the name of Niambale. I say call, but it wasn't a phone call. It was a young kid who had run all the way to the village I was serving in so that he could get me because his father was sick. Now, I'd never been to this village yet because they'd made it clear they wanted nothing to do with me. I was barely tolerated in the village I was in." He laughed, coughed, and then laughed again. "Anyway, I put that little messenger on the back of my four-wheeler and I traveled the bumpy, dusty path to Niambale. It took me almost an hour, so no telling how long it took that youngster to run to me, and by the time we reach the village, we can hear the wife wailing. And I'm thinking, no, God, not this.

You give me an entry point to this place, to these people, and the man is already dead? They're not going to believe in you this way, God! They're not going to listen to my message!"

The music stand wobbled beneath Kevin's slight weight, and Galen wished he had something sturdier for the man to lean on, but Kevin didn't seem to notice.

"But that's what we disciples do, isn't it? We doubt! We're a bunch of Thomases, not trusting in God's plan! So, I didn't know what to do. Part of me wanted to just turn around and drive away, but I knew I should at least comfort the widow. So I let the little boy pull me into his little hut and there his father lay on a small, low bed. I could tell the boy wanted me to do something for his father, so I knelt beside him and put my hand on his arm, which is when I realized he was still warm. Now, the mother is still crying, and I look at the man's chest, and he's not breathing, so I put my fingers on his wrist to check for a pulse, and I can't find one. I tip the man's head back to give CPR, and as I do, I cry out, "Help me, God!" and I don't even get my mouth to his before the man draws in a breath.

Kevin pauses to let that sink in. "That's all I said, friends. I said, 'Help me, God!' It wasn't a fancy prayer. But that little boy and that woman heard it, and they gave it credit. The woman rushed to her husband, who, after a few rasping attempts, started to breathe normally. And a few minutes later, he sat up and started speaking. He had no memory of dying, but he believed that he had. He said he'd known he was going to.

"Friends, I learned something that day. I learned that the miracle-working God of the Bible hasn't gone anywhere, hasn't changed. We are just getting in the way. With our faster-than-light technology, our screens, and our info zipping across the planet at all times. We turn to every other thing before we turn to God. We turn to doubt before we turn to God. There in that village, God was all I had. I didn't even have hope. I had a desperate plea, and I shot it out!"

Galen wanted very badly to see if the people behind him seemed to be buying this story. He was having trouble buying it himself. Was Kevin *sure* the man had been dead? Maybe he'd just been unconscious. It would still be a miraculous story.

"You can doubt me if you want. Thousands of people have heard this story, and thousands have doubted it, and that's okay. But if you want a miracle-working God in your life, you need to get your doubts out of the way. You need to get yourselves out of the way. You need to stop doubting and start believing in the God who can do anything he wants. He can heal. He can transform. He can resurrect people from the dead." Kevin gave Galen a little nod to let him know he was done, and Galen went up front to welcome Blanktified back to the stage.

Chapter 25

Galen

Kevin covered for Galen on Sunday morning, so that Galen could teach at his own church, and Galen was discouraged when Howard and Ruby Jackson did not come walking through the doors. In fact, no one did. Every single person in attendance at Open Door Church that morning lived in either the sanctuary or the parsonage. The Udis had been wrong. Putting up a revival tent on the other side of town had not brought people into his church. What were the Udis doing that he wasn't doing? What was he doing wrong? Maybe his wife was right. Maybe it was time to give up. As he shared the Gospel message with his guests, he tried to prepare himself for this reality. If this was what God wanted, then he would do it. He would walk away.

When Galen got to Curl Up and Dye, Kevin's car was the only one in the parking lot. The salon wasn't open on Sundays, and that was okay because it hadn't exactly brought him a lot of traffic the day before. Phyllis hadn't even bothered to walk into her own backyard to hear her nephew play.

Galen found Kevin sitting in the front row reading his Bible. He was hesitant to interrupt.

"Good morning!" Kevin said when he saw him.

"Morning. Thanks so much for covering for me. Thank you for everything you've done. I don't want to think about how this would have gone if you hadn't been here to help me. But you can go now. I don't expect much to happen today, and you've done enough."

"Are the kids coming back?"

"They are." Though Galen had thought about telling them not to bother. "They were going to go to church first, but I've got them scheduled for another set at three."

"That's good. I think this has been good for them. And you're right. I'm a bit spent. I think I'll go home and take a nap, but I'll come back and check on you later. You still planning to go till seven?"

"That was the plan." The plan was now to sit alone in the tent until The Tent Shop people showed up to take it away.

"How was church?"

Galen sat down beside him. "Business as usual, I guess. Two people said the salvation prayer for the first time."

"You sound disappointed."

Had he? He hadn't meant to.

"Were you expecting a bigger number?"

134

Galen tipped his head back and looked at the tent ceiling. *It's going to get hot under here today.* "No, that's pretty much par for the course. But I don't get as excited about that as I used to." He stopped. He couldn't believe he'd just said that aloud, to Kevin McLaughlin of all people. "Sorry. That sounded horrible. What I mean is, a lot of our guests come to the altar and say the prayer, but then have no interest in discipleship, no interest in seeking more of God, no interest in changing anything about their lives. They ask for forgiveness on Sunday morning and then go get drunk on Sunday night." He almost didn't dare look at Kevin, but he had to know if the man was horrified.

Kevin nodded somberly. "I'm sorry to hear that, but I can't say I'm surprised. Still, it doesn't mean that it's all for naught. Some of those people will allow discipleship and change later." He paused. "And you're right, some won't. But all we can do is the job God gives us, and leave the rest up to him."

Galen had heard these words, or ones just like them, so often, they had no effect on him. "I know."

"How is your wife?"

That was random. "My wife? She's fine. Why?"

"Oh, no reason. I was just thinking that I really like her. You got a good one there, Galen. And I wondered why she didn't come around much yesterday. Wanted to make sure she was okay."

"She's okay," Galen said quickly. "She was running the shelter while I was gone. One of us tries to be there at all times, in case someone new shows up and needs help, or in case the cops come to arrest a murderer. You know, stuff like that."

Kevin was staring at him, and Galen fought the urge to squirm under his gaze.

"You have been given a tough row to hoe. I thought the homeless people helped out some too?"

"They do, sometimes, but we don't have anyone right now that we can trust in the office, except Harry, who is only trustworthy half the time."

Kevin laughed. "Yes, I like Harry." He paused, looking contemplative. "I can see why you wanted to do this tent meeting. You guys are both doing too much. You know, you can't run on an empty tank."

"My tank's not empty." Why was he feeling defensive again?

"And how's your wife's tank?"

What? What kind of a question was that? Was he supposed to know the answer? He didn't say anything.

Kevin stood and faced Galen, leaning on his cane with both hands. "Sometimes, revival starts in surprising places."

Chapter 26

Galen

Two o'clock. Galen felt like crying. It was time to face facts. This wasn't working. Nothing he did worked anymore. Maybe he had run his course and it was time for someone else to take over. Or maybe the shelter itself had run its course.

Either way, it was time to surrender this to God. Of course, he had done that before. He'd said the words, told God that he would do whatever God wanted him to do. But had he really let go? The blisters on his fingers suggested he still had a pretty tight grip on the reins.

There was no altar in the tent but Galen went and knelt in front of the short stage. "God, I give up," he said aloud. "I've asked you show me what you want, and I thought this was it. I thought the tent flyer and the check meant that you wanted me to put this thing up, but I can see now that I must have misunderstood. Can you please make your will plainer to me, and if not your whole will, then what you want for my next step? I don't want to have another heart attack. I don't want to have to wrestle another murderer to the floor all by myself. I'm too tired for this … I'm too tired to ask for a big picture solution, I think." As Galen talked, he gained a better understanding of his own feelings. "If you want to show me anything at all, please show me a tiny step, something I can do. Please give me a tiny sign for a tiny step." Galen remembered Kevin's story from the day before and cried out the same prayer now. "Help me, God!"

Kneeling no longer seemed sufficient. Galen was too tired. Grateful there was no one there to see, Galen pivoted to the right and went the rest of the way to the ground. Lying prostrate before his God, a new gratitude washed over him. Yes, he was still discouraged and he had no idea what he was supposed to do next, but what a journey it had been! He smiled into the grass, remembering all the victories God had given them, all the people whose lives really had changed, all the people who had been healed, remembering a young boy named Daniel who had grown into such a mighty young man of God because of that church, because of God and what God did through that church, the many bellies that had been filled, the many hearts that had been changed. There had been success stories. Galen had just forgotten them amidst all the sob stories.

But now, overcome with gratefulness, he thanked God for every success story he could remember: the man who had been healed of blindness; Shannon, the mother of three, who had found Jesus, got her life together and gone back to school to become a teacher; Marcus, who had gotten sober and was now an Alcoholics Anonymous sponsor to countless other men; Esther, who had found Jesus at the Open Door altar and then shared him with her children who had shared him with their children and a whole family had chosen to follow Jesus. He stopped praying and rested in that feeling of contentment for a long time. Eventually, he thought he should probably get up in case someone did show up, think he was dead, and call 911 again. But before he pulled himself up, he thought he should ask for that small sign one more time. "Please, Father, just show me the next step. Just show me what to do right now. Thank you, Father. Thank you for everything." As he picked his head up, he knew something had changed. He thought then that he was done with Open Door, that God was about to transition him to something new and different, and he knew that it would be okay. That whatever God had planned would be okay.

He opened his eyes and found he was being watched. He locked eyes with those of a chickadee, which was standing about ten feet away, staring at him. *Better than a turkey vulture*, he thought, and started to do a push-up, but the chickadee stopped him with a cry: "Ma-gee." Wait. What? He'd heard a chickadee's call before. About a million times. He'd never thought one was saying his wife's name, though. He shook his head and looked again at the bird. And the bird sang again, clear as day, two high-pitched syllables: *mag* and *eeee.*

He brought himself into a sit, still staring at the bird. It sounded like a chickadee always sounded, but at the same time, it sounded as though it was singing his wife's name. Suddenly, his heart ached for her. He wished so much that she were there with him, hearing this. He scrambled to get his phone out, hoping that the bird would sing again, so that he could record it and share it with his wife, but as he pressed the video button, the bird took flight and fluttered out of sight. Disappointed but not surprised, Galen leaned back on his hands and thought about what he'd just heard. Was that his sign? Was God saying something about Maggie? And hadn't

Kevin also said something about Maggie? A thousand thoughts flitted around his mind and he struggled to put them into an order that made sense.

He didn't get far, though, because a familiar voice interrupted his reflection.

"Where is everybody? I thought this was supposed to be a revival?"

He didn't have to look to know who it was. Gertrude had arrived.

Chapter 27

Maggie

Harry had finally returned to the church and, after scolding him for abandoning the tent revival, and missing a required Bible study and a required Sunday service, Maggie asked him to cover the office so she could go check on her husband.

Galen had seemed downright depressed when he'd left the church, and she was worried about him. She didn't know what she was going to do about it, but something had to give. He was going to have another heart attack if something didn't change.

She invited the boys, and only Elijah wanted to come, so she left Isaiah behind with his video games and she and her youngest drove across town to Curl Up and Dye.

There were cars in the parking lot! Only a few, but there were cars! So maybe he wasn't sitting alone being depressed after all. She waited for Elijah to get out of the car, and then together they strode across the gravel lot. They hadn't reached the edge of the grass when the silence exploded into a Skillet song. Galen had found their early tapes, or Blanktified was attempting a cover song. Either way, it was *loud*.

Elijah picked up his pace, and she tried to keep up.

She found four teens on the stage, a cluster of people near the back of the tent, and her husband on the far side talking to none other than Gertrude. Wonders never ceased. Maggie headed their way as Elijah found a seat.

"Gertrude!" Maggie hollered and leaned over Gertrude's walker to give her a hug, which Gertrude shrank away from. "It's so good to see you! I thought you'd moved to South Dakota!" It occurred to Maggie that this was why Gertrude used a walker—to avoid hugs.

"I have!" Gertrude hollered back, offering no explanation as to why, if she lived in South Dakota, she was standing in Mattawooptock. Had she come back just for the tent meeting? Maggie wouldn't put it past her.

"How are things going?" Maggie asked.

"Just dandy!" Gertrude hollered. She looked at the band and then added, "Why are they so loud?"

Maggie didn't know how to answer that, and Galen didn't seem interested in trying to answer that, so the three of them just stood there until Gertrude said, "I can't take it anymore! Call me if anyone gets killed!" She turned her walker away from them and slowly trudged away.

Maggie looked at Galen, wide-eyed. "What is that supposed to mean?"

Galen looked her in the eye, and butterflies skittered across her stomach. There was something different about him. Or about the way he was looking at her. Or both. "You know, she thinks she's a detective, so if there's a crime, she wants us to call her."

"Oh! Is that why she was here? Because of Damien?"

Galen grinned. "She didn't say as much, but she did ask a lot of questions about the incident."

Maggie shook her head. "But they've already got the guy!"

Galen shrugged. "Crime might be slow in South Dakota."

Blanktified finished their song, and the pocket of people in the back erupted in applause. Maggie realized then that those were the Blanktified fans. She gave them another look. The Blanktified *parents*. Those were definitely parents, with a few grudging siblings mixed in. "Do they do a lot of cover songs?"

145

He shook his head. "That is the first one I've heard. I think they're getting sick of their own songs. They've done the same set every time." He hurried to add, "Which is fine because no one has been here to hear them."

Maggie snickered. "Except Gertrude."

"Right. Except Gertrude." He folded his arms across his chest. "I didn't realize how much I'd missed her until I saw her, and then, when we got talking, I realized I didn't miss her so much after all."

Maggie laughed. She wanted to hug her husband then, but didn't. It felt awkward. When had that happened? When had she become afraid to touch her own husband? She didn't know. She thought it had been a gradual change, but she wasn't even sure of that much.

Blanktified started up another song.

"Do you want to sit?" Galen hollered.

She nodded, and he led her to the front row.

Blanktified was horrible, but they sure were earnest, and Maggie appreciated their verve.

"May I hold your hand?"

What? Her eyes snapped toward her husband. She nodded quickly. Of course he could. She reached for his hand and intertwined her fingers with his. What was this? He hadn't held her hand in over a decade, and back when he'd used to hold it, he hadn't asked permission. But maybe he felt awkward about touching her the same as she did about touching him. She tried not to stare at him, but she wanted to. What had happened between the end of their church service and now? It was hotter than the blazes under that tent; still, she appreciated the warmth of his hand in hers. Whatever had happened, she was grateful for it.

She waited an entire song before looking at him, and then she allowed herself a peek at his profile, which was as handsome as ever, at his T-shirt, which was tighter than it used to be, at the silver flecks on the side of his head. How she loved this man. After all these years, he still took her breath away. She wished that she could still have the same effect on him.

Chapter 28

Galen

Galen didn't want to let go of his wife's hand. It had taken all the courage he could muster to grab it in the first place. But, unless he was going to drag her up front with him, he had to let go.

Why can't you take her up front with you? he asked himself, and he didn't know the answer. So he did. When Blanktified had finished their final set, he rose to his feet and didn't let go of Maggie. He didn't pull her, so she had a chance to decline the silent invitation if she wanted to, but she didn't. She went with him to the front, and he didn't bother stepping up onto the stage.

He saw then that Kevin had returned from his nap, and Galen gave him a broad smile. "I can't thank you all enough for what you've done here this weekend. I think it goes without saying that we didn't get the results we were hoping for, but I have a sense of peace about the whole thing that I can't really explain. I'm disappointed, of course, that a million people didn't come and find Jesus, but I'm so grateful that I got to spend some time listening to and talking with Kevin McLaughlin, and I'm equally grateful that I've gotten to know the members of Blanktified a little, and gotten to listen to their art. I know some crusty old pastors like to bemoan the future of the church"—Maggie giggled and a couple Blanktified moms joined her—"but I don't think they have anything to worry about, as long as the church is full of talented young people like you guys. I am truly, truly grateful for your service here, and I thank you." He took a breath. "I'm going to hang around for a few more hours, just because this thing is supposed to keep going until seven, and if someone wants to show up for the grand finale, I want to be here, but you guys can definitely go." He smiled and then started to return to his seat.

"Do we have to?" lead singer Todd called out.

Galen furrowed his brow. Did they have to what?

"Do we have to leave?" Todd clarified.

Galen shook his head quickly. "No, of course not."

"We could play another set?"

Why did they want to play another set to an almost-empty tent?

One of the fathers started to protest, and Todd gave him a distinctively teenage look.

"You guys don't have to stay. You've heard these songs before."

That father's expression suggested this was an understatement.

"But we can still stay." Todd looked at his bandmates, who quickly nodded their confirmation. Then he looked at Galen. "If you want us to."

Galen opened his mouth to respond, but that father was now standing and looking put out.

"I think maybe Pastor wants a break from all the music." The father's tone fell a little shy of supportive.

"Not at all," Galen said. "It's up to you parents, of course, but I would love to listen to another set. They're welcome to stay and play as long as they want." He looked at the kids. "If someone shows up, I may pause you so that I can share the Gospel." They nodded. Everyone under that tent knew that wasn't going to happen.

Maggie was giving him an incredulous look. He was glad he was still able to surprise her.

"Can we?" Todd asked one of the women.

She nodded and went to give him a kiss on his cheek. He didn't dodge the kiss, but he did look at the ground, and his cheeks grew pink.

Then she left the tent, and all the Blanktified groupies followed. Galen swept an arm toward the small platform. "The stage is yours."

"Actually, Pastor, we wanted to ask you something." For the first time, Todd looked nervous. He looked at his sister, his eyes begging her to interfere, which she did.

"You have, like, a mandatory Bible study every night at the shelter, right?"

What, were they thinking of moving in? Galen nodded.

"And you have worship music then?"

Galen nodded again. Not exactly. Years ago, they'd had full bands and concert-level music. Now, sometimes they had Harry. Sometimes they sang along with downloaded tracks. But he didn't get into specifics.

"Well," Alexandra continued, "we were wondering if we could volunteer to lead worship sometimes, like maybe once a week?"

Part of Galen was overjoyed at this offer. Help? Yes! But part of Galen was skeptical. While Galen believed that nearly any song could be a worship song, these kids' music fell a little left of worship music expectations.

Alexandra read his mind. "We *can* play more traditional stuff. We just prefer the good stuff. But maybe we could lead your people in worship, and then maybe close the service out with one of our originals?" She looked so hopeful. Even if he'd wanted to say no, he would have struggled to say no to that face.

But he didn't want to say no. He swung an arm toward the stage again. "Show us what you got."

As he and Maggie took their seats, still hand in hand, the teens eagerly returned to their instruments and after a long, excessively loud intro from their drummer, they brought their instruments' volume down as Alexandra leaned into the microphone, and loudly and clearly, sang the first line of "Raise a Hallelujah" in a smooth, strong alto. Galen's jaw dropped and he snapped it shut. No need to wear his shock on his face, though the kids probably wouldn't see it because they all had their eyes closed. Todd joined his voice with hers on the chorus, and a chill danced up Galen's spine.

"Oh my goodness," Maggie breathed, "they're *not* terrible."

"No, they are a far cry from terrible."

Chapter 29

Maggie

Maggie could smell the coffee before she stepped into the kitchen. Galen must have made it. No way were her boys up yet. During summer vacation, they slept as late as possible. And even if they were up, what were the chances one of them would think to make her coffee? It wasn't unusual for Galen to make coffee, but he usually had already made it, drank it, and left the house before she got up.

She stepped into the kitchen to find him at the stove. What on earth? "Coffee?" she asked.

He whirled around, spatula in hand. "Yes. And not the cheap kind you've been buying either. I went out and got the good stuff." He pulled the pot out of its slot and poured some into a mug. Who was this, and what had he done with her husband? He started to hand her the mug and then hesitated. "Sorry, do you still take cream and sugar?"

She nodded, a small giggle escaping her as she slid onto a stool. "Yeah, it hasn't been that long."

His face flushed. "Well, I know how you've been trying to be healthy lately."

Actually, her health kick had ended about a year ago, but she wasn't going to correct him. Might be time to start it up again anyway, now that her young husband was having heart attacks. "Thank you." She picked up the mug and blew over its brim.

He put the coffee pot back and then looked at her, and she felt self-conscious. She wished she'd put on real clothes. Or combed her hair. Or brushed her teeth. Any combination of these things. She pulled her frayed robe a little tighter around her. "What?" She couldn't stand his gaze.

"You're beautiful." He delivered the words sans emotion, as if it was an objective observation, something that was so obvious it didn't even need to be said.

"Thank you," she managed, but she could hardly breathe.

"So, I've been thinking ..." He leaned on the counter and stared out the window. "This might sound weird, or goofy, or whatever, so please say no if you don't want to. It was just a thought ..."

"What?" She couldn't stand the suspense.

"What would you think about doing devotions together in the mornings?"

She snickered, and then clapped a hand over her mouth, really wishing that snicker hadn't sounded as derisive as it had. "Sure!" she said quickly, to make up for the snicker.

He looked skeptical. "Really?"

"Really. Yeah." Had he lost his mind? What was going on?

"You say yes, but your body language suggests it's a goofy idea."

"No, no," she said quickly. "I'm just surprised is all. Where is this coming from?" She meant all of it: the coffee, the compliments, the devotions, but she would settle for an explanation of the last part.

He stood up straight, gripping the edge of the bar with his hands. He seemed to be searching for words, and she wished she hadn't demanded any.

"You might think I'm crazy ..." he finally started.

When had that ever stopped him from sharing before?

"I just feel like God wants me to focus on your spiritual wellbeing right now."

Her spine transformed into an iron rod. "Beg your pardon?"

His face fell, and he held up one hand. "No, that's not what I meant. Obviously, you're spiritually healthy. You're the most spiritually healthy person I know. I just … I just … well, Kevin said something about our gas tanks …"

What? This was because of Kevin?

He let go of the bar with one hand so he could furiously rub his palm into his eye socket. "I sure am butchering this. So, he said that maybe I was running on an empty tank, and of course, he's right, and then he said maybe you were running on an empty tank too, and I felt awful because I hadn't really been thinking about that." He took a breath, and the rod in her back relaxed—a little. "I'm sorry. I've been jumping from one crisis to the next, and I haven't really taken the time to think about our own well-being because there's always another crisis."

He looked at her with his big chocolate eyes, and what was left of the rod in her back melted away. She wanted to reach across the counter and take one of his hands, but she couldn't quite make herself. "I love you," she said instead. Words were easier than touching these days.

"I know you do, and I am so, so grateful. You can't imagine how grateful I am. And I'm sorry that, when faced with heart failure, my decision was to jump headlong into a new project, a project that had me falling flat on my face." He looked down at the counter. "Literally," he mumbled, and she wondered if he'd done a face plant trying to cross that bumpy Curl Up and Dye field. He raised his eyes without raising his head. "I honestly thought that's what God wanted me to do. I'm still confused as to those signs. Those couldn't have been coincidences."

"It's like the sled principle," a small voice piped up from the bottom of the stairs.

Maggie turned to see Elijah standing there in his pajamas, his hair stuck up in the air. "The what principle?"

Elijah approached the counter, looking at the stove. "Are you cooking something, Dad?" He sounded shocked.

"Yes!" Galen spun toward the stove and turned off the burner. "I almost forgot!" He picked up the frying pan and turned toward them. "Does anybody want some burned corned beef hash?"

"Yes!" Elijah said without hesitation. "I like it when the bottom is all black and crispy."

Maggie shuddered at the thought, but was glad someone was willing to accept Galen's offering, so that she didn't have to.

Galen slid a patty of hash onto a plate and then slid that across the bar to his son, who got up to get his own fork. "What's the sled principle, Elijah?"

"It was in this book I was reading. A man has to move to a new town, but he has all this stuff to take with him, and only one horse. So, God tells the man to build a sled." He sat back down and cut off a giant chunk of hash.

"That's going to be hot!" Maggie warned, and Elijah refrained from shoving it in his mouth.

"Maybe I should get some juice." He started to get up.

"I'll get it for you," Galen said. "You keep talking."

Maggie couldn't remember the last time Galen had gotten a beverage for one of his sons. Or encouraged one of them to keep talking.

"So the horse tries to pull the sled, but he can't, and the guy hollers at God, 'Why did you let me build a sled?' and then he gets the idea of wheels. So he builds two wheels, puts them on the sled, and has a wagon. Now the horse can pull all the guy's stuff, and the guy says to God, 'Why didn't you just tell me that in the first place? Why have me build a sled?' and

God says, 'I had to let you build the sled so you could get to the next step. You never would've gotten to the wheels if I didn't let you go in the wrong direction for a few steps.'" He shoved that giant bite into his mouth and then quickly followed it with some orange juice.

Galen leaned on the counter again, staring at his son, seeming to not follow.

"So, you're saying that God had your dad put up a tent just to get him to the next step?"

Elijah nodded and swallowed. "Maybe. If Dad suddenly thinks of some wheels, then we'll know that the tent meeting was the sled."

Chapter 30

Galen

Galen couldn't believe he was nervous about morning devotions, but he was. He'd already been up for an hour, had already done his prayer-walk, and was now sitting on his couch with his Bible, trying to figure out how to do a morning devotion with his wife. He felt entirely unprepared. He didn't want to preach at her. Exactly how did couples do devotions? He knew this was a thing. Maybe he should've asked Kevin. He thought about texting him, but was too embarrassed.

He looked up as he heard Maggie coming down the stairs. Her hair was wet from the shower and she was already dressed. This surprised him. Usually she had her coffee before she got ready for the day. "I made you coffee again," he said, sounding too much like a bad pupil trying to kiss up to the teacher.

"Thank you," she said graciously. "I'll be right back." She glided into the kitchen and got herself some coffee and then returned to set it on the coffee table. "Hang on, I forgot my Bible."

He watched her walk up the stairs, and silently thanked God for her. He hadn't been appreciating her enough lately. He hadn't had the time or energy. Or rather, he hadn't *made* the time and *reserved* the energy.

She came back down the stairs and sat beside him, seeming a bit tentative.

"So, I'll be honest," he started. "I don't really know how this is going to go. I've led a lot of devotions over the years, but usually, I just read a Scripture and then talk about it. But I don't want to preach to you." He chuckled and leaned back into the sofa. "Do you want to preach to me?"

She seemed to be considering it. "I don't think so."

"Okay, so how do you want this to go?"

She let out a long breath.

"I'm sorry. You were probably expecting me to be better prepared."

"No, no, that's not it. But I don't know how it's supposed to go either. Maybe we could just read some verses and then pray? And if we do this every day, certainly it will get less awkward." She smiled at him. "We'll get better at it."

"Yeah, yeah, that's a great idea. Okay, so what Scripture?" He opened his Bible.

She shrugged. "I like to do the open flop method?"

He looked up at her. "Huh?"

"I'll show you." She held her Bible out in front of her with both hands. "Father, show me what you want me to see." She gave the slender book a small shake and then relaxed her hands, and it wobbled a bit before falling open. She looked down.

"Okay, where are we at?"

She looked up at him, a bit of chagrin in her eyes. "It doesn't always work. We're in Ecclesiastes." She started to close the Bible, but he stuck his hand out over hers and kept it open.

He laughed, a genuine laugh that felt foreign to his chest, but relaxed him from head to toe. "That's okay. What does Ecclesiastes have to say to us this morning?"

She read, "There is an appointed time for everything. And there is a time for every event under heaven—A time to give birth and a time to die; A time to plant and a time to uproot what is planted—" She looked up at him. "Is this God telling us to uproot ourselves from here?

He thought maybe that this was exactly what was happening. They were certainly deeply rooted there. Their family had been birthed at Open Door. Galen had the urge to tell her about that stupid chickadee. "I don't know. Keep reading."

She'd held her place with her finger. "A time to kill and a time to heal; A time to tear down and a time to build up. A time to weep and a time to laugh." She looked up again. "Remember when we used to laugh together, about all the craziness of this place? When did we stop laughing?"

He didn't know, but it had been a while ago. He reached out and put his hand on her knee. "That's a good question."

"A time to mourn and a time to dance. A time to throw stones and a time to gather stones." She looked up quickly, her brows scrunched together. "It's just occurred to me. Is that stones for building or for throwing at others?"

He would have laughed, but she looked so serious. "My understanding is that it is the throwing away or the gathering of stones for building."

She nodded somberly, and kept on. "A time to embrace and a time to shun embracing. A time to search and a time to give up as lost; A time to keep and a time to throw away. A time to tear apart and a time to sew together; A time to be silent and a time to speak." Her voice changed then, as if she were choked up. "A time to love and a time to hate; A time for war and a time for peace." She looked up and closed her Bible, bookmarking the spot with one finger. "If this is God telling us what to do, I am so confused."

He laughed, slid closer to her, and kissed her on the temple. "Me too. I think we should pray."

Chapter 31

Maggie

Elijah stuck his head into the church office, where Maggie was attempting to pay bills. "Have you seen Dad?"

She tipped her head toward his office, but then thought she should follow Elijah in. They'd just gotten their third copy of their overdue oil bill from spring, and she wanted to ask Galen if he had any new ideas about how they were going to pay it.

She let Elijah ask his question first. "Are you coming to my game tonight? It's a big one, against Skowhegan."

She found it interesting that he'd even asked. Usually, her boys just assumed their dad would be too busy to come. But Galen had been different the past few days, hadn't he? Maybe Elijah sensed a change.

"Sorry, bud. I've got an appointment to see Damien Foll tonight."

Nope, not that different.

Elijah dropped his head—disappointed, but not surprised.

"I'm really sorry. I made the appointment days ago, and it's hard to get those visits scheduled, but … When is your next game?"

Elijah looked to his mom for help.

"Saturday, I think." Without referencing her calendar app, she had no idea. "I'll have to double-check."

Galen nodded. "Okay, listen up, Elijah. Unless I'm so sick or so injured that I can't move, I promise to be there."

Definitely different. Galen didn't break promises, and he didn't make promises that he didn't plan to keep. Elijah seemed to know that on some level and bounced out of the office, satisfied with the answer he'd gotten.

Galen looked at her. "Sorry, I really think God wants me to go see Damien."

She wasn't so sure about that, but she nodded. "Okay."

"I should have asked you about Elijah's schedule before I made the appointment."

Her breath caught. That wasn't something he would normally say. When she found her voice, she said, "No, it's okay. We only found out about it yesterday. They do everything last minute." She didn't try to hide her annoyance with that fact.

He nodded. "You'd think our family would work well with that method."

She moved a pile of paper so she could sit in a chair facing him. "We do work well with that method, but that doesn't mean it isn't stressful. Anyway, the oil company is not happy with us right now." She held up the bill.

He groaned and leaned his head back. "I forgot all about that. Yes, I've got to figure that out. I'll call them again, try to explain."

She knew that he'd already made this call at least once, and didn't envy him the task of doing it again. "Are you sure you want to go see Damien? I mean, is it safe?"

Galen chuckled and rubbed his jaw. "You know I've been to visit people in jail before."

He'd done it a lot. "Yes, but ..." She wasn't sure why she was so uncomfortable with the idea. "But Damien is ... he's a murderer."

Galen folded his hands in front of him on his cluttered desk. "Is he, really, though? Or was he out of his mind with drugs?"

She didn't know. But he'd killed a man. He was a murderer.

"All I know is, God still loves that child of his, and I'm going to go tell him that. I don't know if Damien will want to hear that, or if he'll even be able to hear that, but someone needs to say it to him. And everyone I've heard from has been so angry, so hateful toward him because of who he killed, well ... I'm just not sure anyone else is talking to him about God's love."

Maggie let his words settle. "So, it has to be you?"

"Probably not. If I said no, God would probably send someone else. But I think he's sending me this time."

She couldn't disagree. She wasn't confident that he was wrong. She got up to leave, but found she really didn't want to. She walked around the desk, not even sure what she was going to say or do when she got to him. She stopped in front of him, and he looked up at her expectantly. "Can I just give you a hug?" she asked, her voice cracking at the end of her question.

"Of course." He jumped up and wrapped one of his thick arms around her waist. With his other hand, he pulled her to his chest, and she nuzzled into his neck. He felt so warm, so safe, so familiar. She didn't want to move out of that hug, and he didn't ask her to.

Chapter 32

Daniel

Ember hid from Daniel for a few days, refusing to return his texts, and he worked not to worry about her. If she wanted to date creepy old men, what business was it of his?

Then one afternoon, he was sitting on his fire escape when he realized she was staring up at him. He gave her a little wave.

"Are you alone?" she called up.

He thought she meant alone on the fire escape and he nodded. Of course he was alone. The fire escape wasn't that big— couldn't she see he was the only one on it?

"I'll be right up!"

As she ascended, he figured she'd probably meant to ask if his mom and Martin were home. Yes, he was also alone in this sense. He watched her climb, trying not to get too excited. She was probably just bored. Or wanted something.

"Hey." She arrived, out of breath, and plopped down beside him, so close they were touching. She stuck her legs out through the slats. "It's too far up here." She wiped her forehead with the back of her hand. Then she leaned back and stuck her chin to her shoulder, giving him a coquettish look. "But I suppose you're worth it."

"What's up?" he asked, softening the question he was really asking: *What do you want?*

"Not much. What's up with you?"

He leaned away from her a few inches. "Why haven't you answered my texts?"

"Yeah." She managed to sound remorseful. "I'm sorry. I've had a lot going on. Been kind of …"

Though he gave her time, she didn't finish that thought. "Kind of what?"

She let out a long breath. "I don't know. I can't handle life right now."

That didn't explain anything. He reached behind him. "You want a beer? They're warm."

"No thanks," she said quickly, surprising him. She'd never turned down a beer.

He cracked one open. "Why?"

She gave a shrug that was almost imperceptible because she was leaning on her arms. "I dunno. Just not in the mood."

Since when? "Okay." He took a long drink off his. It was pretty gross and he had to work to swallow it. He didn't even like beer.

"Do you ever think about what's right and wrong?"

His eyes snapped toward her. What was going on with her? "Uh … sometimes."

"How do you decide?"

What? What did she think he was, a pastor? "Uh … can you be more specific?"

"You're saying it depends on the circumstances? Like some things aren't always wrong or always right?"

He didn't know what to say, and he didn't like thinking about this stuff. It reminded him of the little boy he used to be. The stupid, naive little church boy. He took another long drink. "I don't know."

She elbowed him playfully. "Yes, you *do* know. That's why I'm asking." She gave him a chance to say something, but when he opted not to, she kept going. "You know I'm not usually worried about morals and everything, but … but what if someone does something wrong, something that can't be undone? Like, something that is serious. You know what? Never mind." She started to get up.

"Wait." He didn't want to have this conversation, but he didn't want her to leave either. "You're thinking about doing something that can't be undone?"

She shrugged again, and her bare, tan shoulders looked so soft, he desperately wanted to touch them.

He forced himself to focus. "Are you or not?"

"It's hypothetical."

Her shoulders looked less tempting. He had moved past grumpy to officially annoyed. "Are you thinking about getting a tattoo?"

She laughed shrilly, and her eyes sparkled with joy. She was so beautiful. "No, but that's not a bad idea! We should go get some together! We could get matching tats."

He chuckled and took another drink. "Like what?"

"I don't know, something sweet … like bunnies or something."

He was not going to get a bunny tattoo, even for Ember. "I don't know, Ember. I don't think I care enough about hypotheticals to come up with an answer, but I would say that if you, my friend, were thinking about doing something that you knew was wrong, something that you can't undo, then I would ask you what the consequences would be, and if they would be worth it—"

"I don't know if it's wrong. That's what I'm asking you."

"Well, I don't know if this mystery sin is wrong or not if you don't tell me what it is." He hadn't meant to use the word *sin* and was deeply embarrassed that he'd done so. He took another swig and finally felt the beer hit his brain. *It's about time.*

She was staring at him. He sensed that she really wanted to tell him whatever it was she was dancing around. Why didn't she, then? "You know that you can tell me anything. I'm not going to judge you, ever."

Her eyes got wet and she looked away. "You'd judge this."

Chapter 33

Galen

Galen stepped up to the dirty plastic window. "I have a visitation appointment with Damien Foll." He slid his driver's license into the drawer.

The impassive woman pulled the drawer shut, examined his license, and then gave him a stoic nod that said, *Wait for an indeterminate amount of time*. He returned his wallet to his back pocket, a little annoyed that they held his license hostage during these visits. He didn't understand how that benefited them. He sat down near a worn-looking woman, who gave him side-eye. He smiled at her, which made her even more suspicious. He checked the time on his phone and then, to kill some minutes, opened a social media app. Then he had a thought. Why not text something thoughtful to Maggie? Would she like that? Would she think he was weird? Would it alarm her? Why did the idea of texting his wife cause so many doubts to run through his head? He tapped on her name and wrote, "I love you." Then, before he could have any more doubts, he hit send.

Immediately, "Are you okay?" came back, and he silent-snickered.

"Absolutely. Just wanted to tell you. I don't think I tell you enough."

There was a longer delay this time, but as the corrections officer unlocked the visitors' door, she answered, "Thank you. I love you too."

There. That hadn't been so hard, had it? He didn't know if the chickadee had been a sign from God. He didn't know if the chickadee had really said, "Maggie," but it sure couldn't hurt to take better care of his wife.

He had always thought that marriage time and family time were things he had to sacrifice in order to minister to all those he was supposed to be ministering to.

Now, he wasn't so sure.

He motioned toward the door, allowing the tired-looking woman to enter the tiny visitors' room first, and then followed her in. The corrections officer closed the door behind them. Through the dirty window, Galen saw a much healthier version of Damien looking back at him. Ironic that incarceration looked good on him. Galen set his Bible on the small shelf in front of him and sat down on a stool that was bolted to the floor. He wished he could slide it back a few inches, but if wishes were horses, and all that.

He picked up the filthy phone and forced a smile.

After nearly a full minute, Damien picked up the phone on his side.

Galen listened to the robot tell Damien to enter his inmate ID number and then listened to the beeps as Damien slowly did so. Galen wished there was a way to do all this that didn't involve turning human beings into numbers. The robot told them both that this call would be recorded and then a soft buzz told them both that the line was open. Galen took a breath. "You look better, Damien."

Damien grunted.

Galen waited for him to say words.

He didn't.

"How are you feeling?"

Damien didn't answer, at first.

This might be a short visit.

"How do you think I'm feeling?"

"I don't know," Galen said quickly, and then forced himself to slow down, take the edge out of his voice, knowing Christ wouldn't already be frustrated with this guy. "That's why I asked."

He grunted again.

"You look a lot better. I assume you've got some sobriety time under your belt, now?"

Damien looked down at his free hand. "Not by choice."

"It still counts, though, and the longer you're sober, the better you'll feel."

Damien's upper lip pulled up. "I don't think I'm ever going to feel good in here."

Galen was already very tired of this conversation. "Damien, do you know why you're in here?" Galen gave him ample time to respond, but he didn't. "I think it might be healthy for you to think about that."

He sneered. "Healthy?"

Yeah, maybe that hadn't been the best word to use. "You currently have a set of circumstances. Do you want to make the best of those circumstances?"

"I want to get out of here," he almost growled.

"I don't think that's likely."

"Why did you come here?" Damien raised his voice, then looked around as if he was expecting to be clubbed for it, and lowered it again, all in the space of those five words.

"I came here because God loves you, and I love you, and I want to help you."

He grimaced, but didn't say anything.

"How can I help you, Damien?"

177

He hesitated. "You could put money in my commissary."

"I don't have any money. What else can I do?"

Damien stared at him. "Nothing. I don't want nothing from you."

This was going so well. Galen was so happy he wasn't in the bleachers with his wife watching his son play basketball. "Can I share some Scripture with you?" He worked very hard to put love in his voice.

"No thanks."

The man sitting two stools over from Damien began to holler at the tired woman, and she shrank back from his anger, but she didn't let go of the phone. Galen tried to keep one eye on her, just in case, and one eye on Damien. "Damien, I can only imagine what you're going through right now, but I promise you, God wants to help you. He loves you, and he wants to help you."

Nothing.

The other man came to his feet, and even though there was no way he could get to the woman on the other side of the fake glass, Galen came to his feet too, instinctively. But he didn't need to. As the angry man in a jumpsuit pounded on the window and swore at the woman, two guards rushed into the room and pulled him out. Galen looked at the woman, who was now in tears. "Are you okay?" A stupid question, probably, but the only one he had. She didn't answer, and he settled back on his stool.

"Don't bother sitting down, preacher man. We're done here." Damien threw his phone at the window, and it bounced off with such efficiency, Galen wondered if the window was partly made of rubber. Damien stood and turned toward the door, pounded on it, and then disappeared, leaving a speechless Galen squatting over his stool, half standing, half sitting, looking and feeling foolish. He stood back up and followed the tired woman to the security window, where she was waiting to get her ID back.

"Is there anything I can do to help you?" he asked softly.

She shook her head, the tears still falling.

He handed her his card. "If there ever is, please give me a call or come by my church."

She looked down at the card as if it were a slithering snake and then up into his face. "Are you hitting on me or something?"

He laughed and then wished he hadn't. "No, ma'am. I'm a pastor, a happily married pastor.

I can tell you're hurting, and God loves you, so I want to help you, if I can."

The security officer appeared on the other side of the window and opened the drawer, revealing their two licenses, side by side. She snatched the card out of his hand.

"I'm Galen, but most people call me G."

"Moriah," she said without looking at him. She reached for her license and then headed for the door.

He followed her lead.

When they stepped outside, the wind nearly knocked them over. It had been a blazing hot day, and the sun was going down. Galen checked the sky for thunderheads, but they were surrounded by tall buildings, so he couldn't see much. "Are you okay to get where you're going?"

She looked at him suspiciously.

"I mean, do you need a ride?"

She shook her head, looking disgusted, and walked away.

Feeling an emptiness that wasn't quite discouragement, Galen turned toward the parking lot. He remembered the early years, when such a sequence of events *would* have discouraged him, but somehow, he was beyond that. He had become numb to it. He'd stopped expecting miracles, stopped expecting things to change, stopped expecting people to want God's love. Is this what Kevin had been talking about? Had Galen become a doubting Thomas? He didn't think so. *I've just become a realist,* he thought as he slammed the truck door. But then another thought came: Does God want realists? Galen didn't know, but he suspected that maybe God didn't. God operated in the miraculous supernatural, didn't he? So maybe he didn't want his servants expecting the natural, expecting their version of reality to trump God's version of reality.

Galen leaned forward and put his head on the steering wheel as small balls of hail began to ping off his windshield. "God, I am so tired. Please fill me. Please fill me with your supernatural power. Please let me live in your version of reality, not mine." He waited there, with his head on the wheel, waiting for something—tongues of fire or descending doves—anything other than what he had. But nothing came. Only the mighty rushing winds of the approaching thunderstorm and the falling balls of ice. He started the engine and drove away, keeping an eye out for the poor woman who'd just been screamed at by a man in an orange jumpsuit.

Chapter 34

Galen

The balls of ice grew bigger and then turned to giant splatting raindrops as Galen drove. The winds were fierce and he considered pulling his truck over and waiting for it to pass, but he wanted to get home. So he drove. He turned onto 201 and saw a Lincoln pulled over on the shoulder with an obviously flat back tire. He groaned and slowed to a stop. Then he backed up and eased his truck in front of the car. He didn't really want to change a tire in the rain, but he felt nostalgic for the days when he did this all the time, when this was his job, when this was his service. Life had been simpler then.

He climbed out of the truck, wishing he had a coat, and was instantly drenched. At least it wasn't hailing anymore. He squinted, trying to see if there was anyone in the car. And then he saw that there was. Ruby Jackson. Oh boy, this should be fun. He approached the window, which she rolled down. She looked scared, and he was suddenly eager to comfort her.

"Hi, Mrs. Jackson. Nice day out, huh?" He smiled, trying to be charming.

She still looked petrified.

"If you pop the trunk, I'll get your spare on and get you on your way."

"Really?" She looked up at him as if he'd just offered to perform brain surgery.

"Yes, ma'am. Easy peasy." He headed for the trunk, in a hurry to get this over with and get home.

"Oh, thank you so much." She opened the door and her key started chiming. "I don't know how to thank—"

"No need!" he hollered over his shoulder, trying to be heard over the wind. He saw she was following him. "You don't need to get out, Ruby," he said, dropping the last name formality. "I can get this for you. You can stay in the car and stay dry." As he said the words, he realized they were silly. She was already drenched.

She used her fob to open the trunk, and he lifted the lid to peer inside. Good grief, that was a lot of stuff. "Sorry, I've been meaning to stop at The Salvation Army. But I always drive the stuff around in my trunk for a month or so first." She laughed nervously, or was she just cold?

"Do you mind if I dig for the tire?" he asked, his head inside the trunk.

"Of course not. Do you want me to move some of the stuff to the backseat?"

"No, no, I got it." He located the jack and pulled it out, standing up straight and looking down at the woman, who looked smaller and frailer now that she was soaked. "Are you sure you don't want to wait in the car, at least try to stay dry?"

She raised her penciled eyebrows at him, and it occurred to him that those might wash off. "Are you trying to get rid of me?"

He laughed, a genuine laugh. "No, ma'am." He squatted in front of her flat and started to loosen the lug nuts. "Do you know what happened?" It looked like a new tire.

"I do not. I was driving along and my tire light came on. I had only just pulled over when you showed up. I think God sent you."

Good. It was about time God had sent him some place someone actually wanted him to be. "Maybe."

"I saw you walking out of the jail." Another question lay beneath the surface of this one: *Why were you at the jail?*

"Yes, I was visiting Damien Foll."

He thought he heard her gasp, but he couldn't be sure over the wind. He looked up at her and saw her hand was over her chest. Yep, she'd probably gasped.

"Why on earth were you doing that?"

Was she serious? "Well, you know, 'Remember the prisoners' and all that." He tried not to sound defensive and almost succeeded.

"Isn't that verse referring to other believers held in prison because of persecution?"

He glanced up at her, surprised. Maybe this woman did know her stuff. "Maybe." He really needed to focus on what his hands were doing, so he could get out of the rain. He got on all fours to set the jack. The mud soaking through his jeans felt like ice water.

"That man murdered a police officer." She wasn't going to let it go.

"Yes, he did, but he was out of his mind on drugs at the time." Galen didn't know this for sure, but he somehow knew it just the same.

"Well"—she managed to sound hoity-toity, even standing there in the downpour—"does that mean he's showing remorse?"

Galen chose not to answer that question, and went back to the trunk to get the spare tire. "How about 'I was in prison and you visited me'?"

It was her turn to choose silence.

He returned with the spare and knelt in the mud to finish his job.

"Yes, maybe you have a point."

Thank God for small victories. Because that's all he'd been having lately.

Chapter 35

Galen

The following morning, Galen and Maggie spent devotional time together again. Galen found it awesome how quickly this had become a routine. It had lost its awkwardness, and now he looked forward to it. Maggie seemed to be enjoying herself too. Still, when Maggie left the couch to go do some haircuts, Galen felt less than encouraged. He leaned back into the cushions and closed his eyes. "Is this really all there is, God? I put up your tent. I'm focusing on Maggie. And we're still struggling to feed the people staying at our church. I still don't know how to pay that fuel bill, and I don't know how much longer the fuel company is going to wait. I hate that an unpaid bill is tarnishing your reputation, Father. Please, do something! I guess I don't need a big revival. I guess I'm just asking for a little movement, somewhere. Please! Show me the wheels!"

Galen had the idea to go to his knees. He didn't know if the suggestion had come from his own head or elsewhere, but he obeyed it. He went to his knees on his own living room rug and waited. He didn't know what he was waiting for, but he waited, trying to be patient, trying to focus on God and not let the million other thoughts stampeding through his head distract him.

Nothing happened.

The minutes ticked by, his legs cramped, and nothing happened. Isaiah came down the stairs and started at the sight.

With some difficulty, Galen rose to his feet. "Sorry, didn't mean to scare you. I was just praying."

Isaiah didn't say anything. He only stared at his dad for several seconds and then went into the kitchen. Galen followed him, suddenly hungry.

The next morning, Galen tried again. He got up early, walked around the church property praying, came inside to make more coffee for Maggie, had morning devotions with her, and then went back to his knees, asking God to do something, to change something, to give him some supernatural guidance, to fill him with some supernatural power. He waited and he waited, meditating on *Cease striving and know that I am God.* And nothing happened.

Morning number three, Galen went through his routine and then went to his knees. And he waited. And he waited. On his knees with his head bowed, he waited. Then he got the urge to put his hands in the air, and he obeyed that urge, and in a heartbeat, he felt something akin to electricity hit his fingertips, travel down his arms, and fill his torso. He almost yanked his arms down at the shock of it. It felt like heat, like energy, like power. He'd never felt anything like it before and tears came to his eyes. The feeling left his arms, but it had settled firmly in the rest of him. He lowered his arms, rocking forward and letting out a small sob. When his body continued to fall forward, he let it, until his forehead hit the floor. He laughed then, imagining how he must look. "What was that, God?" he muttered into the floor. At first, there was no response, but then a message traveled through his mind. He could see it, traveling on a script in front of his closed eyes, like a banner being towed by an airplane. It even appeared to be rippling in the wind. It said, "That was what you've been asking for."

He sat up with a start, eyes wide open. Instantly, the doubts came for him. He'd imagined it all. There had been no energy.

There had been no message. He had wanted something so bad that his mind had conjured it up. But he knew these doubts were lies, and he tried to bat them away. "Father, I don't know what I'm doing," he said, feeling weaker than he'd ever felt.

The answer came as a soft, inaudible whisper. "Good."

He rose to his feet and looked around his empty living room. What was he supposed to do now? He looked at the rug, and considered going back to his knees. It had been more comfortable there.

His phone rang. The resting was over. The work was about to begin.

Chapter 36

Galen

It was the Somerset County Jail calling. Damien Foll had tried to commit suicide. He was now in the infirmary and asking for the pastor from the homeless shelter church.

Of course he was.

Galen texted Maggie to let her know where he was going and why, and then he climbed into his truck. It started on the first try, and as was his habit, he thanked God aloud for this.

When he walked into the jail, he expected to be whisked off to the infirmary, but instead, the woman behind the dirty window had no idea what he was doing there. He explained it twice and then gave up, and she, looking peeved, said she would find someone else to ask. She left him standing there in the small, stuffy lobby, disappointed he wouldn't get to see the jail infirmary. He'd been curious.

After fifteen minutes, he took a seat, and it seemed it was that very act that summoned a corrections officer to the room with a key. The large man unlocked the door for him and ushered Galen into the room, where Damien sat waiting, already holding the phone.

Galen forced a smile and picked up the phone.

Damien punched in his number and then thanked Galen for coming.

This visit was going to be different. "You're welcome. I'm really glad to see that you're still alive."

Something resembling a smile flitted across Damien's face. "I need help."

Yep. You and everyone else I encounter.

He lowered his voice a little. "Spiritual help."

That sounded more interesting. "Go on."

"I almost died, and when I did, I saw some stuff."

Galen waited.

"I can't describe it. I can't even remember it, really. It's fading like a nightmare. Except it wasn't a nightmare. It was too scary to be a nightmare."

Galen believed him. He could hear the fear in his voice, as well as something heavier than fear—a resignation to reality, maybe? He'd discovered something about this life, and he wasn't bothering to argue against it. "What do you remember?"

He shook his head. "I don't really want to talk about it. You'll think I'm crazy, and I don't want to think about it too much. But there was pain, and this awful emptiness. I was so alone. And worse, I could see a small light, but it was so far away. I wanted to reach for that light, but I couldn't." He paused, swallowed hard. "It was like it was off limits, and I knew it. And I was alone. Forever. I changed my mind. I didn't want to die. And then they brought me back. I'm so glad they found me when they did. I will do anything, Pastor, *anything* to make sure I never feel that way again. I think I died. I think I was on my way to hell, and I don't want to go to hell."

Galen nodded. "You don't have to. All you need to do is ask God for forgiveness and then follow Jesus."

He nodded emphatically. "Yes. I already asked for a Bible, and I was reading it till they called me down."

Wow. "Great. Have you prayed yet?"

He shook his head. "I don't really dare to. I can't imagine how mad God must be at me."

"Okay, let's pray now. Do you want me to lead you in the prayer?"

He nodded, fear all over his face.

Galen wished he could touch him, try to comfort him, but all he could do was bow his head. "Father, I thank you for Damien. I thank you for what he's just gone through so that he could learn your truth before it was too late." Galen led Damien through a prayer for salvation, and Damien repeated every word. Galen had never heard anyone sound so sincere. "Go ahead and add anything you want to, Damien. And you don't have to do it aloud if you don't want to."

Damien started mumbling, and Galen could hardly make out the words. Then Damien burst into tears and just kept saying *sorry* over and over again. Galen heard him say Klaus's name and tears came to his eyes too. Silently, he thanked God for letting him be part of this. He hadn't wanted to come down to the jail the first time, let alone the second, but now he was so grateful that he had, that God had chosen him for this, that he was witnessing real transformation.

Damien stopped talking and wiped his face on the inside of his coveralls. Then he looked up with bloodshot eyes. "I feel so weird."

Galen nodded. "You're a new creation, as of right now, Damien. Welcome to the kingdom of God."

"Now what do I do?"

Galen hesitated. Damien's future was chock-full of spiritual hope, but he still lived in a physical world, where he had recently murdered a man. "Now you seek God. That means that you try to get to know him on a personal level. You do this by reading and studying his Word, your Bible. Are you a good reader?"

"I used to be."

"Good. That will make it easier. I can get you some other books to help you understand the Bible, but the Bible is the most important book. And pray. You can talk to God anytime about anything. And don't just talk. Listen too. And then you'll want to talk to other believers. I can come see you, and they offer Bible studies here. Just try to live every day for God, and even though you're in here, you will see positive change. God will help you make the best of your circumstances. He will probably use you to help others."

Damien snorted. "Seriously?"

"Seriously. There are a lot of people in there with you who need God, and he will use your testimony to keep others—"

"My testimony?" Damien asked, alarmed.

"Yes. Your personal story. He will use it to keep others from going to hell."

Damien looked down at his hands, appearing to be in deep thought. Without looking up, he asked, "What do I do about the trial?" Galen didn't know what he meant. As he was trying to figure out the right question to ask, Damien clarified. "I pled not guilty, and that's the plan for trial. But I am guilty." He paused. "Do I have to plead guilty?" His voice wavered.

Galen's shoulders were almost too heavy to hold up. "God always wants us to tell the truth. I would ask God that question, and then listen for his answer. And his answer might come to you while you're reading your Bible."

Damien's Adam's apple bobbed up and down. "I don't want to plead guilty."

"I know. Sometimes God asks us to do hard things."

Chapter 37

Galen

It had been years since Galen had gotten excited about a Sunday morning service, but he was excited this morning. He didn't know why, but a weird energy was coursing through him.

"Do we do devotions on Sunday too?" his wife asked him on her way down the stairs.

"I think we should, if you're up for it."

"I am. Just let me get my go-go juice." She headed toward the coffee pot. She'd come to expect that he'd already have it made for her, and he kind of liked this expectation.

They settled in together on the couch and he reached for his Bible.

"I was thinking about a verse I'd like to use today," she said, sounding tentative.

He was thrilled. "Of course! What is it?"

She gave him a cute smile. "You're in a good mood today! What gives?"

"I don't know. I guess I'm just excited about church." He felt this needed an explanation, though he didn't exactly have one. "I guess I'm just excited to share Damien's story." He hurried to add, "He gave me permission."

She leaned in and gave him a kiss on the cheek and his stomach filled with butterflies.

This surprised him. This wasn't exactly their first date. He tried to get a grip as he waited for her to get her verse.

"It's 2 Chronicles," she said, sounding apologetic. "It just came to me this morning." She began to read, "Then the Lord appeared to Solomon at night and said to him, 'I have heard your prayer and have chosen this place for Myself as a house of sacrifice.'" Her emphasis of the words *this place* sent a chill up Galen's back. "'If I shut up the heavens so that there is no rain, or if I command the locust to devour the land, or if I send pestilence among My people, and My people who are called by My name humble themselves and pray and seek My Face and turn from their wicked ways, then I will hear from heaven, will forgive their sin and will heal their land. Now my eyes will be open and My ears attentive to the prayer offered in this place.'" Again, she emphasized *this place.* "There's more, but that's the gist of it." She reached out and put her hand on top of his. "I know you were disappointed about the tent turnout."

Was he? He hadn't even thought of that in days, but yes, he had been disappointed.

"But I think revival can happen right here. It might not look like a million people getting saved. In fact, I don't think it will. I think we can't even imagine how it will look, but I also think it's already started. Damien? … *Us?*"

He didn't really know what she meant by *us*, but the word froze him. Did his wife think that they needed revival? As in their family? Their marriage? Did his wife not know how much he loved her? He didn't think about it—he just slid toward her, grabbed her with one hand and pulled her close, and then he kissed her like he hadn't kissed her in years. Not just a hello peck or a goodbye peck or a good night peck, but a real kiss, the way a man kisses the woman he loves. She reached for his cheek and kissed him back and he thought he might melt into a puddle right there on the couch.

"Oh gross!" Isaiah exclaimed from the stairs. "Why don't you two get a room!"

Galen pulled away from her, a foolish grin on his face. "Son," he said, without looking away from his wife. "You need to start praying right now that God sends you a wife like your mom." He glanced up in time to see Isaiah's eyes roll. He didn't care, though. He gave his wife another kiss and then said, "I'm going to head over to the sanctuary. I've got the urge to pray over the service. But I can't thank you enough for being my wife. I love you so much.

And I am so grateful that you are you." He wasn't sure this made sense, but she looked happy, and he rose to his feet on shaky legs. Then, with a bounce in his step, he walked out of his house and into his church.

Chapter 38

Maggie

Maggie couldn't believe what had just happened. Her husband still loved her! Really loved her! There had been more passion in that kiss than anything she'd experienced in *years*. She was giddy with excitement and relief. They were going to be okay. Whether they left the church or not, their family would be okay. She knew it now.

She jumped into the shower, eager to join her husband in the sanctuary, even though the service didn't start for another few hours. Technically, they still offered Sunday school, so she always tried to get there in time for that, even though they rarely held class anymore. They didn't require the guests' children to attend Sunday school, and no one from outside the church came, so usually she filled up that time working in the office.

Today was different. She walked into the sanctuary to find four well-groomed children sitting quietly together in a pew. Where on earth had they come from? She soon solved the mystery. Her husband was at the front of the church, talking to a couple she didn't know. She approached tentatively, not wanting to interrupt.

Galen's face lit up when he saw her. "Ah! This is my lovely wife, Maggie. She pretty much runs the logistics of the shelter. I run around putting out spiritual fires, but she makes sure everyone has a bed and food. She keeps families together and separates those who need to be separated."

This wasn't exactly praise, but his tone made it sound that way, and she relished it. If she gathered together all the praise she'd received in the last five years, it would have fit in a tablespoon.

"All alone?" the woman asked.

"I have some help," Maggie said, thinking of Harry, whom she hadn't seen in days.

"Yes. She does it alone," Galen said. "Maggie, this is Ruby and Howard Jackson. They have recently moved to the area to be near their grandchildren." His eyes flitted to the row of well-behaved children.

"Yes, and our son. He and his wife should be here shortly. They wanted to sleep through Sunday school."

Sunday school! "Did the kids want to go? I can head downstairs right now and get started."

Ruby waved the thought away with a white gloved hand. "No, no, it's all right. Galen has explained to us that you haven't been doing Sunday school lately. Maybe next week."

Did that mean she was going to bring her grandchildren again next week? This was a miracle in itself!

Galen's eyes darted to the door, and she heard him gasp. "Kevin! Hey!" He left the Howards to go greet the senior missionary.

Maggie's mind worked a mile a minute to think of something to say to the Howards, so they wouldn't feel Galen had abandoned them. It turned out that she didn't need to say anything because Ruby was in a chatty mood.

Ruby lowered her voice. "I've got to say, I was so skeptical about this place when I first heard about it. To be honest, I was more than skeptical. But when your husband stopped to change my tire in a torrential downpour, I knew he was the real deal. I could see it in his eyes. He'd been ministering to a murderer and then he stopped to help me when he could have driven on by." She stopped to draw a long breath. "I'll admit, I am not yet comfortable around the home—" She stopped herself. "Around people who live here. But I think God wants me to get more comfortable."

Maggie noticed then that they were both wearing very nice, probably expensive clothes.

"Or he at least wants me to get more comfortable being uncomfortable." She tittered. "We've prayed about it and have received very strong instructions that God wants us to serve here." She held her hands out to her sides, palms up. "So, use us. We are here to serve."

Maggie's eyes filled with tears. She was speechless.

But this was apparently okay because Ruby left her to go greet Kevin. Maggie followed her in time to hear the tail end of Kevin's announcement that God had told him to start serving at Open Door Church. Did Galen need any help leading the Bible studies? He would be happy to do every weeknight except for Thursdays, when he had bowling league.

As Galen gratefully, and a little breathlessly, accepted this offer, Elijah's basketball coach came through the door, with his son in tow. Maggie had heard Galen invite him to church at Elijah's game the night before, but never in a million years did she think he'd actually show up. Maggie was on her way to greet and welcome him when a storm of teenagers and musical instruments came through the door, followed by several parents and siblings.

Maggie stepped in close to her husband. "I didn't know they were coming today," she whispered.

"I didn't either, until this morning. Todd texted me and asked if they could. Said God told him to."

Maggie had to sit down. God sure was sending out a lot of instructions lately. She bowed her head and tried to thank him, but she couldn't utter a single word.

Chapter 39

Galen

Galen watched from the back of the sanctuary as Blanktified finished up their set and Kevin McLaughlin stepped behind the music stand that Galen used as a lectern. The teens settled into the front row, which was a surprise to Galen. He'd figured they'd bolt after their set, but they appeared to plan on staying for all of Monday night Bible study at the homeless shelter.

Galen didn't have to stay, but habits were hard to break, and he wanted to hear what Kevin had to say. As Kevin began to speak, Maggie and the boys slid into the pew beside him. He couldn't remember the last time they'd all attended a weeknight service. Maggie gave him a broad smile and took his hand, and he couldn't believe how much he loved her.

Kevin introduced himself, giving only a brief rundown of his resume, seeming to read his audience well. These guys and gals wouldn't be impressed with all of Kevin's years in Africa. They could scarcely understand what it even meant. He told them that he'd be taking on some of the weeknight Bible studies and that if they had any questions for him at any time, to give him a call. Then he shared an announcement with them. "I know it's the end of July, and you guys probably aren't worried about heat right now, but God is planning ahead, and today he performed an awesome miracle on your behalf." He paused to build the suspense, but his audience didn't seem to care. Still, he continued, "While I'm sure that you specific individuals will no longer be here come fall and winter"—Harry would still be there, Galen thought, and probably several others—"but those people who will be here will be toasty warm because today God paid for the entire winter's supply of fuel."

A murmur traveled through the small crowd. "What does that mean?" Lily fired from the back. "Who bought the fuel?"

"God did. He sent one of his faithful servants to pay the fuel company. Isn't it awesome to be used like that? Would *you* like to be used by that?" He had their attention.

He'd left out parts of the story, of course. How they hadn't yet paid for their last delivery in the spring, and how the fuel company had informed them that for the coming winter, they wouldn't deliver any oil unless it was paid for in advance. This had irked Galen, who had never been late on a bill in eight years, except for this one. But Howard Jackson had taken it in stride and simply paid the outstanding bill and then asked how much oil they'd used the previous winter and paid for that much again. Galen was miles beyond grateful. In a Maine winter, nothing was more important to the homeless than not being cold.

Galen had thanked Howard and Ruby over and over until Howard shushed him. "That's what we're here for."

Galen hadn't known that the Jacksons were wealthy when they'd walked into his revival tent, and he still didn't know how wealthy they were, but he'd seen their tithe check, and he'd heard the amount they'd given the fuel company. They were certainly better off than anyone else Galen had ever known. And he couldn't stop thanking God for them.

Kevin read Ephesians 2:10 and then went through a list of practical, realistic ways that God could use the people in the sanctuary, and most of them continued to listen to him. Galen was impressed at how well he was targeting his audience.

He asked them to bow their heads, and most of them did, and Kevin waved Blanktified back onto the platform, where they started to softly play a hymn. Wonders never ceased. Galen couldn't decide which of the many miracles of the last few days surprised him the most. Then Kevin gave an altar call and six people went down front. Galen blinked twice. One of them was Harry.

Harry had heard countless altar calls in his seven and a half years as a guest at Open Door. He'd responded to a few. But this time, something was different. He didn't walk down front with his shoulders slumped. He *rushed* to the altar and threw himself to his knees in front of it.

Things were changing.

And after the sanctuary had emptied, after his family had gone home, and after Galen had thanked Kevin and told him good night, Galen made a trip of his own to the altar. Though a great part of him wanted to join his family in the parsonage, a greater part of him had an overwhelming desire to pray. He went to his knees.

It was not lost on him that those old knees of his had gotten more of a workout in the last week than they'd had in years. But they continued to serve him well. The minutes ticked by and turned into an hour, and still, Galen prayed. He ignored the buzzing phone in his pocket and it wasn't until his wife returned to the sanctuary and put a hand on his shoulder that he finally looked up.

"You okay?" she asked, her eyes full of concern.

"I'm so much better than okay." Pushing off on the altar, he brought himself to a stand. Then he took his wife's hand. "Let's go home."

Chapter 40

Maggie

It had been years since Maggie had felt the urge to attend a weeknight Bible study, and she couldn't remember the last time she'd attended two in a row, but she couldn't stay away. Tuesday night found her back in the pews, excited to see what would happen. Galen would be speaking that night, and Blanktified had the night off, so she suspected the service wouldn't be quite as dynamic as the night before had been.

She was wrong.

Elijah's basketball coach was back, and he'd brought his girlfriend and her kids. He said he couldn't stop thinking about God and wanted to learn as much as he could as fast as he could.

Harry didn't show up, which was totally against the rules, but Lily asked Galen if she could try her hand at the piano. No, she'd never had a lesson, and no, she hadn't tried before. Maggie was certain it would be a bad idea, but Lily had been one of the people at the altar the night before, and it appeared that Galen didn't want to discourage her because he didn't say no.

Maggie braced herself as she knew that piano hadn't been played in years, but it turned out the bracing was unnecessary. Somehow, Lily's hands danced over the keys and a song they all recognized came out. The motley congregation stood and most of them began to sing. God did not touch their voices the way he had touched Lily's hands, but the discordant lyrics were beautiful anyway. Did they understand what they were singing? Maggie wasn't sure that they did, but a greater percentage of them were singing, and many of them had their hands up in the air. Lily played song after song, and the majority of the people sang along.

When Galen finally stepped up front, the congregants sat down and looked at him expectantly. "I know I'm supposed to teach you something right now, but I asked God for a verse, and he gave me 1 Thessalonians 5:17. Do any of you know that verse?" He didn't give them much time to answer. "It's only three words." He held up three fingers. "Pray without ceasing." He closed his fist. "That's what he gave me, and that's what I think we should do. Will you all pray with me for a few minutes? Ask God for whatever you need. Ask him to heal your bodies. To heal your relationships with your families. Ask him to get you a home, if that's what you want. Ask him to get you out of this place. I know there's a lot of work to do around here, but right now I think we're just supposed to pray." He glanced at her, and there was a spark in his eyes she wasn't familiar with.

She was a little disappointed. She wanted to hear him speak, and she knew the coach and his people hadn't shown up for a prayer meeting, but she tried to trust Galen's judgment, and she bowed her head to pray. She prayed for her sons, for their health and protection, for their future wives. She prayed for the guests at the church, that each of them would choose Jesus, would find a home of their own. And she prayed for her husband, a prayer that caused her to soon run out of words. Then she sat there quietly, waiting for words to come.

One of the guests gave up and left the room. She peeked up to see if Galen was going to respond, to tell the man that he had to stay until the service was over, but Galen didn't even seem to notice that someone had left. She glanced at the coach, who was holding the woman beside him, whose body was racked with sobs. Maggie went to her without hesitation, sliding into the pew behind her. She placed a soft hand on her shoulder and began to pray quietly. The woman's crying intensified and Maggie forced herself to be patient and keep praying. The woman would talk to her if she wanted to.

Harry walked into the sanctuary, looked around bewildered, and then went straight to the altar. Several men and one child followed his lead. The sanctuary was full of crying, praying people.

There was hope in the air.

Chapter 41

Galen

On Wednesday evening, Galen was almost nervous to walk into the sanctuary. His brain was sprinting to catch up with and process all that had happened. He now only had a handful of guests at the shelter who had not chosen Jesus. He had never, in all his years, had a shelter full of heaven-bound people and yet now he believed it was possible. More than possible. Likely.

Wobbly legs carried him into the large room where he had spent so much of his life. His wife was already sitting in one of the middle pews, and he slid in beside her. "Where are the boys?"

"They wanted to go watch TV," she whispered.

He was disappointed, but he couldn't blame them.

It was Kevin's turn to lead Bible study and he showed up with fire in his pockets. Galen didn't think he knew what had gone on during the previous service, and yet he chose to speak on the power of prayer. He then asked for prayer requests, received a remarkably long list, and then began a long corporate prayer. Much to Galen's surprise, most of the guests stuck with him and prayed for the full forty-six minutes it took to work their way through the list. Kevin said, "Amen," and then asked Harry to come up front and lead them in some worship. Lily asked if she could help, and Harry winced, but no one stopped her. This turned out to be a good thing. Lily's playing brought Harry's up a level, whether Harry was aware of that or not.

There was no invitation and still the pews emptied as people went to the altar. Galen's breath caught. He couldn't believe what he was seeing. He turned to see Keem still sitting in the row across the aisle from him. He looked grumpy. Galen tried to catch his eye so he could offer a smile, but Keem wouldn't look at him. Because Galen was staring off to his right, he didn't see Kevin approaching. When Galen saw him, he jumped. The man was standing directly in front of him. He'd leaned his cane against the pew so he could reach out toward him with both hands. For a split second, Galen thought he meant to strangle him, but then the gnarled hands found the top of Galen's head.

"God's given you something to say," Kevin said.

Galen did not doubt this, and yet was unprepared for the bolt of energy that traveled down through his body, from Kevin's hands to his own toes.

"Get yourself out of the way, son," Kevin said softly but firmly.

Galen rose to his feet, and as if his mouth had a mind of its own, it opened and declared something—loud and firm and incomprehensible. Instantly, Galen felt self-conscious. What had he just done? What had he just said? Everyone was staring at him—especially Keem Deqow, whose mouth had fallen open. Unsure of what else he could do, Galen sank back into his pew.

Kevin was staring at Keem. "What is it, son?"

Galen tried to shake his head at Kevin, but it felt too heavy to move. There was no use in asking Keem anything. He could barely understand any English, let alone speak it. Keem took his phone out of his pocket and began to type furiously.

Galen looked at Kevin, "What was that?" he asked, sounding hoarse.

Kevin grinned broadly. "That was God, son." He grabbed his cane and started toward the front of the church, but Keem chased him down the aisle, holding his phone out in front of him. He grabbed Kevin's arm and Kevin slowly turned to face him. Keem stabbed at something on his phone's screen and a robotic voice said, "He spoke Somali."

Kevin looked down at the phone, looked at Keem, grabbed him by the shoulder, gave him a good shake, said, "Well, I'll be," and then looked at Galen, who still didn't understand what had just happened.

Keem stabbed at his phone some more and then held it up. "The time is now for salvation," the robot voice announced. Another few stabs and "That's what he said in Somali."

Galen exhaled as the realization of what had just happened washed over him. He looked at Maggie, worried she would think he'd lost his mind, but her expression suggested no such thing. Tears spilled out of her eyes as she mouthed, "Wow" to him.

"Yeah. Wow," he said.

She pointed toward the altar and Galen looked to see that Keem had just gone to his knees in front of it. There were no language barriers when God was around.

Chapter 42

Daniel

Thursday brought a break in the heat wave, so of course, Martin announced that he was taking Daniel and his mom to the beach. This was weird, and there was always a catch with Martin, but even if there wasn't a catch, Daniel would have rather dined on rusty nails than spend time with either of them, so he said he was going to the store and then never went back to the apartment. He headed toward the Back Cove and texted Ember on the way, asking if she wanted to join him in making fun of the tourists. She didn't answer for a long time and he had given up on her when his phone beeped. "I'm in Libbytown. Can you come get me?"

Come get her? What did she think, he'd suddenly grown a car? "Come get you? Like on foot?"

Her only answer was the street address. Yes, apparently, she wanted him to come on foot. It didn't matter. He would walk to the moon for her and she knew it, so he headed southwest, hoping his mom wasn't driving around looking for him. Just in case she was, he cut through Deering Oaks Park and tried to stay off the main streets. In this way, he arrived at a sketchy looking apartment building thirty minutes later. He knocked on the door, heard some yelling inside, and was just putting his hand to the doorknob when the door flew open and Ember flew out.

"Let's go!" she cried.

He looked behind her, ready for a fight, but no one seemed to be chasing her. "What's wrong?" He followed her down the steps and then the street.

"Nothing. I just want to be somewhere else."

He didn't understand, but he hurried to catch up to her. "Hang on, slow down, I don't feel like going for a jog today."

"Where are we going?" she asked.

"How should I know? You're the one leading! Whose place was that?"

She looked at him and he saw the bruise under her right eye.

"Whoa ..." He stopped walking.

She took his hand and tugged him forward. "Come on, let's go to the park."

"Who did that to you? Was it the guy in the car? Was that his place?"

She didn't answer, just kept pulling him down the street. They finally made it to the park and she paused to lean against the tree. He thought about asking her to sit, but the ground at their feet was littered with garbage and broken glass. "Let's go sit on that bench."

She looked at the bench, glanced around like a scared rabbit, and then nodded.

He led her to the bench, sat down, and put his arm around her. "If you don't tell me what's going on, I'm going to lose my mind."

She whimpered. "I don't know where to start."

"At the beginning?"

She sneered. "Well, I was born. That was my first mistake."

He pulled her into him. "Don't say that. I'm very happy you were born."

She put a hand on her stomach. "Not if I tell you what I have to tell you, you won't be."

Oh no. This didn't sound good. His stomach tightened. But how bad could it be? What could she tell him that would make him not love her anymore? "Just tell me, Ember." He let go of her, but left his arm behind her. "You'll feel better once it's out in the open."

She didn't speak, just sat there sniffling, making him feel like a helpless dunce.

"Is this about that thing you were talking about? That bad thing you were going to do?" He looked at her, trying to read her mind. "Did you do it?"

"I never wanted to do it," she said quickly, defensively. "My sorry excuse for a mother wanted me to do it, is trying to *make* me do it." She bit her lip and stared into the trees. "And maybe I should, I don't know. But I can't seem to make myself."

He was beyond frustrated. "I love you, Ember, but if you don't tell me what's going on, I can't—"

"You love me?" She was looking up into his eyes, and she looked so vulnerable. She didn't usually look like that. Maybe it was the tears. Or the bruise. Or some combination of it all, but she looked like a fragile flower.

He was desperate to kiss her. "Yes." How could she not know that he loved her?

She looked away. "You won't."

He slapped the bench in frustration. "Just tell me!" He never raised his voice to her, but even he had his limits.

"I'm pregnant," she spat out.

He sighed in relief. Was that all? "I'm sorry to hear that." He turned toward her and took her hand. "But it's not the end of the world. We can make it work. My mom was super young when she had me, and look how good we turned out." He laughed, proud to have gotten a smile out of her. "Your mom want you to get an abortion?"

She nodded, chewing on her lip so hard he was surprised it wasn't bleeding. "She's trying to make me. She tried to force me into the clinic, but I kicked and screamed ..." She pulled her hand out of his. "There's more." She twisted her fingers together like she was trying to pull them off her hands. "It's my uncle."

He didn't understand. "What's your uncle?"

"The man in the car. It's messed up. He says he's in love with me but he forces me. It's gross, I know, but I don't know how to stop it, it's been going on for so long. That's why my mom says I have to kill the baby." Her voice broke and she started to sob. "She says it's going to die anyway, that it will be an inbred freak."

Daniel slid his hand out from behind her and leaned forward, putting his face in his hands. He didn't know what to say. He didn't know what to do.

"I told you. Now I disgust you."

He grabbed both her arms and pulled her into him. "No, you don't. I just don't know what to do." He held her tight and let her cry into his chest. Abortion was wrong, right? But what had happened to her was wrong too. And

223

would the baby be okay? Would it even live? Ember was too young to be a mom. She was too young to take care of herself, let alone a baby. He would help, of course, but he had no idea how to do that.

"I take it you didn't call the cops?" he mumbled into her hair.

"What? Ew! No! I'm not going to admit this to anyone!"

Daniel sighed. He could understand that, but that sorry excuse for a man shouldn't be able to get away with this. He wanted to make sure that didn't happen. But first, he needed to get Ember away from her mother. He didn't know if abortion was right or wrong, but he didn't want anything forced on her. But how was he going to do any of this? He was a stupid, broke kid.

An idea came to him like an instant download. "I don't know what to do," he said again. "But I know where we can go for help. I know people who will know what to do."

She looked up at him, incredulous. "You do? Who?"

He kissed her on top of the head. "We've got to go to Mattawooptock."

She snickered. "Matta*what*?"

"Home. We've got to go home. To church."

She pulled away, staring at him, her mouth open. "To *your* church? To the homeless shelter?"

He nodded. "Trust me. They'll help." He hadn't talked to any of them in years. He didn't even know if Galen was still the pastor. Yet, he knew he was.

"How are we going to get there?"

He shrugged. "We'll walk, try to hitch rides if we can."

"It will take us days to walk there."

Daniel stood up. "Then we'd better get started. I'll protect you." He had no idea how he would do this, how they would do this. He had eighteen dollars in his pocket.

"No!" she cried, standing up too. "I'm not walking to northern Maine in July! Are you crazy?"

He gave her a minute to come to terms with the idea. "Do you have a plan B?"

She didn't answer.

He took her hand. "Then let's go."

"We don't have any money. How are we going to eat?"

"Just trust me. I'll take care of you." He pulled her to the street and they both turned north, hand in hand.

Chapter 43

Galen

Compared to previous nights, the Thursday service was quiet and calm—ordinary even. One of the guests fell asleep in the middle of the Scripture reading and began to snore. This was a common occurrence and Galen only worried about it now because there were so many visitors, none of whom appeared to be homeless. They'd shown up just in time for Bible study. A few of them were Blanktified parents, and Elijah's coach and family were back, but there were also several faces he hadn't seen before.

Galen finished his short message and then gave an altar call, hoping that one or more of the few holdouts would finally surrender their lives, but they didn't. Those who had been coming to the altar a lot lately came again, and Galen thought this was still a good thing. He motioned to Blanktified, asking them to keep playing, and then he walked down the aisle, wanting to talk to the newcomers before they figured the service was never going to end and left.

He stopped at the first couple he came to and stuck out his hand. "Galen Turney. Thanks for joining us tonight." The man and then the woman shook his hand. "I'm Blake Butterfield and this is my wife, Amelia. We pastor a church in Littleton, New Hampshire, and we've been thinking about opening our doors to let people stay in the church." He looked at his wife for confirmation, and she gave it. "So," he continued, "we thought we'd come see how it's done."

Galen was speechless. "Sure," he finally managed after a long, awkward pause. "Just let me know what you need. I'll show you anything I can, answer any questions I can."

"Well, the big one right now," Blake said, "is how to get our congregation on board. We've shared our vision with them, and most of them are ready to run for the hills." He laughed humorlessly.

Galen flashed back to the beginning, when Pastor Dan had first had the idea. "I don't have the answer to that one. I didn't start this place, but the man who did definitely met with some resistance. Lots of people left the church, but he decided doing what God wanted was more important than doing what those people wanted."

Blake looked around the sanctuary. "And yet, it seems you've got plenty of community support now. How did you do that?"

"Prayer." Galen couldn't get the word out fast enough. "Lots and lots of prayer." He didn't tell them he'd also put up a silly tent behind Curl Up and Dye. "Please, stick around, and one of us will give you a tour and answer any questions you have, but I need to go say hi to some people. I'll be back."

They both nodded and Galen returned to the aisle and went to the next face he didn't yet know—a hefty man in a baseball cap and plaid flannel shirt.

Galen introduced himself again and welcomed the man to Open Door.

"Name's Zach. I drive truck through here and I got this urge to stop and I'm so glad I did." He looked at Galen as if they shared some secret, but Galen wasn't sure what it was. "Something powerful is happening here, man. I can feel it, and I can't wait to tell my home church about it. There is power in the air. I can feel the Spirit in this place. I hope you don't mind. I'd like to stop by whenever I'm passing through at the right time."

"Of course not," Galen said, stammering a little. "You're welcome anytime. Where are you from?"

"Massachusetts. I drive truck for White Brothers, so I come through fairly often."

Galen nodded, at a loss for words. He started to excuse himself, but then thought better of it. "Can I pray over you before you go?"

The man nodded eagerly, and Galen put his hand on his back and prayed for Zach. He prayed that God would protect Zach in his travels, that God would protect and bless Zach's family and that God would bring miracle-working power to Zach's home church. After he'd said, "Amen," Zach looked at him with wet eyes and said, "Thanks, man."

Galen left Zach and headed for another couple Maggie was talking to. They said they were vacationing nearby in Bingham, but Bingham wasn't exactly nearby. They were going white water rafting in the morning, but they'd heard about the Open Door weeknight services and had decided to come check one out.

"How did you hear about us?" Maggie asked, as if she could easily believe someone could hear about Open Door and was only asking for clarification.

The couple exchanged concentration frowns, as if they couldn't quite remember who had mentioned Mattawooptock.

"I guess I can't remember," the man said, "but we're so glad we came. This was a wonderful service."

The service had been quite run-of-the-mill. Galen hadn't done anything to make it wonderful. But he wasn't surprised that God had.

Chapter 44

Maggie

Maggie drifted toward the couple Galen had already spoken to. The sanctuary was emptying and they were still standing there as if they had an appointment. She introduced herself and learned that they were Blake and Amelia from New Hampshire.

"This is pretty exciting stuff," Amelia said.

"It is," Maggie agreed, not really knowing what she meant. The crowd at the altar? The homeless shelter? Blanktified's rendition of "My Hope Is Built on Nothing Less"?

"You've got a revival going here!" Amelia said.

Maggie wasn't sure they were there yet. "Maybe?"

"Really?" Amelia raised her eyebrows. "You're telling me people around here are always this excited about Jesus? We want to open a homeless shelter and have been worried it would ruin our church, but that is certainly not the case here." She looked at her husband. "I'm so excited to get home and get to work!" She returned her eyes to Maggie's. "We've been praying for revival for more than a year now. I didn't know that opening a homeless shelter would bring it."

Maggie opened her mouth to argue but then closed it again. That wasn't exactly how it had happened, but she didn't want to discourage them. And how *had* it happened? She hadn't thought about it in those terms, but Amelia was right. They *were* experiencing revival, weren't they? "Well, it's been a long hard road," she tried to explain. "It hasn't always been like this."

"No?" Blake was studying her.

"No. We've struggled to pay the bills and to keep people coming to church here. Our guests can be pretty demanding, and people have gotten worn out and have moved on."

Galen joined them, and Maggie's whole body relaxed. "Would you like a tour?"

Blake nodded. "Sure, but Maggie was just telling us how you got revival started here."

She was? She wasn't so sure that's what she'd been doing.

Galen hesitated, looking to her for help, which she was completely unequipped to give.

"So?" Blake pressed, after an uncomfortably long pause. "How have you gotten people fired up?"

Galen studied his toes for a few seconds and then looked at Blake. "For starters, *we* really didn't do anything. We *did* want revival. I wanted it badly. I've been worried that we were going to have to shut the place down, so I started praying for God to bring people." He paused and stared off at an empty wall. "But he didn't, not at first. And then I felt him"— Maggie could tell her husband was struggling to find the right words. She wished she could help him, but she didn't know what he was going to say—"tell me to focus on my heart, and on my wife's heart, and so I tried to do that." He chuckled. "And it wasn't easy. I had to really get on my knees, literally, and just give up. And then things started happening." He looked at Blake. "Sorry, I'm not doing a very good job of explaining it, but it's been a weird trip. He's brought us people and resources and there's a new ... energy."

"How about that tour?" Amelia rescued him.

"Yes, right this way." He stepped back and motioned for them to take the aisle.

"Would you mind if I went back to the parsonage?" Maggie asked. She'd taken the tour a few times already. "I'd like to check on the boys."

"Of course!" Amelia assured her. "It was so lovely to meet you!"

Blake nodded his agreement and then Maggie was free. Free to go home and put on her pajamas and free to think about what Galen had said. Had God really told him to focus on her heart? She didn't know why that amazed her so. God was in the business of doing amazing things, but she still found herself flabbergasted by that little detail.

The boys were parked in front of the television. "You missed another good one," she said to them, but they didn't look up.

"Good," Isaiah said.

She didn't say anything, but continued to stand in the middle of the living room, and finally Isaiah looked up. "Were we supposed to go?"

She shook her head. "No, but God is doing some amazing stuff around here and I just don't want you guys to miss it. I know you're pastor's kids and all, but you've still got room for spiritual growth, you know."

"I know that, Mom," Isaiah said, irritated. "But I also know we've heard Dad's Bible study lessons a hundred times each."

This was true. Because they had such a turnover of guests, Galen frequently recycled Scriptures and themes. "All right. I love you." She went to each of them and kissed them on the tops of their heads, getting between them and the television to do so. Isaiah closed his eyes and tolerated this affection, but Elijah leaned sideways so he could see the television around her. She laughed through her irritation. "Good night, boys. Thanks for being my sons."

"God didn't give us much choice," Elijah said, but his tone was warm and playful.

Maggie changed into her blessed pajamas and then decided to pray for a while, at least until Galen got home, but five minutes later, she was fast asleep.

Chapter 45

Maggie

At two o'clock on Friday afternoon, the phone in the church office rang.

"Good morn—" Maggie stopped and corrected herself. It had been one of those days. "—afternoon. Open Door Church?"

"Is this Maggie?"

Maggie recognized her old friend's voice immediately. "Harmony! Are you okay?" She knew that she wasn't. She wouldn't be calling if she was.

"I'm fine, but Daniel's gone."

Maggie's body went cold and a weird tingling pierced her fingertips. She rubbed her free hand against her jeans. "What do you mean, gone?"

"I mean gone! He said he was going to the store and he just took off!"

Oh good. He wasn't dead. "How long ago?"

"Yesterday."

"Have you called the police?"

She hesitated. No, she had not. "I know who he's with. This trashy kid named Ember. What kind of a name is that? Anyway, Ember's mom said not to worry and not to call the cops, that she and Ember had a fight and that both kids would be back soon."

Maggie was struggling to follow her line of reasoning. Was Ember a boy or a girl? "Why are you listening to Ember's mom, though? Since when do you listen to anyone? If your kid is missing, you call the police!"

"Stop. Just stop. He could be in trouble. If he's done something wrong, I don't want to call the cops on my own son. Besides, you know how I feel about cops."

She had no idea how Harmony felt about cops. If she'd ever known, she'd since forgotten. She would just call them herself. She picked up a pencil. "What was he wearing when he left the house?"

"I don't know. Jeans and a T-shirt, I guess."

"What color? Any hat?"

"Why are you asking all this? Are you going to come look for him?"

Why had Harmony called her? "Is that what you want us to do?"

She hesitated, then slowly said, "I don't know. I didn't think of that."

"One of us should stay here, but Galen or I could come down and drive around the city, help you look."

"I don't think he's in the city."

"What makes you think that?"

"Because he texted me and told me not to worry, that he had to take Ember somewhere."

"Harmony!" Maggie snapped. "You could have led with that!"

"Sorry! I'm having trouble thinking straight. It still doesn't make it okay! That was yesterday and now he's not returning my texts and his phone goes straight to voice mail, so it's either off or dead. I don't know where he slept last night!"

"What's his phone number?"

"I just told you that his phone's dead!"

Maggie tried not to get angry. How freaked out would she be if Isaiah ran away? "Can you please tell me his number? And what does the other kid look like?" Maggie wrote down everything Harmony said, even though parts of it didn't make sense. Ember was a girl, she'd gotten that much, but how could someone have both long hair and short hair? Had Harmony ever even seen this girl? "You said he might be in trouble with the law—"

"I didn't say that!"

Whatever. "Okay, sorry. But if he were, what might he be mixed up in? Is he involved in some gang or something? Drugs?" Maggie couldn't picture any of that, but she was trying to cover her bases.

"No. He doesn't do any of that stuff, and there are no gangs in Portland, Maggie."

She didn't know if this was true, but she wasn't going to argue. She tried to think of another question to ask. The paper in front of her held precious little information. "Any idea where they were headed?"

"No." Harmony called Ember's mother a few choice words, as if this whole thing were her fault.

"So what can we do to help you?" She still didn't understand why Harmony had called her, unless it was solely to scare her half to death.

"I called you so that you would pray." Her voice cracked and she paused to recover. "Please pray for my baby."

The lump in Maggie's throat grew so thick she couldn't speak. She nodded to no one. Of course she could do that. She'd been praying for Daniel since she found out he'd been conceived.

"You there?"

"Yeah," Maggie managed. "We'll pray." She took a long breath, trying to get herself together. "And if you think of anything else we can do," she said, sounding a little too close to hysterical, "let us know. And let us know if anything changes, or if you hear anything."

"I will. Now hang up and start praying, please." Her voice softened on the last words.

Maggie hung up and then dialed Daniel's number. Predictably, it went to voice mail. "It's Maggie, honey. Just wanted to tell you that I love you. If you need anything, let us know. Please call me back."

Chapter 46

Galen

Galen hung up on Maggie and called the Portland Police Department. He was sitting in his truck in the Walmart parking lot and it was starting to get too hot to tolerate, so he opened his door while he listened to the phone ring. Though he lived nearly a hundred miles north of Portland, this was not the first time he'd had a reason to call their police. After several rings, someone answered and connected him to an officer. Grateful that he had not been put on hold, he explained the situation to the officer, who quickly grew frustrated with his lack of information. Galen didn't even know Harmony's address, but he explained that the mother was reluctant to call, and so he was doing it instead. The officer didn't seem too worried about the two missing kids, but took down all the information and asked Galen to send a recent picture when he could. Galen had many pictures of Daniel. None were recent. He certainly didn't have any of Ember. Not confident that the phone call had done a lick of good, Galen hung up and started to pray for Daniel.

Once he was praying, he realized he was more angry than fearful. What was Daniel thinking? Why would he do this to his mother? The Daniel that Galen knew *wouldn't* do this to his mother. What had gotten into him? He tried to calm his spirit and focus on what he was asking God: to interfere, to protect Daniel and Ember, to bring them home.

His phone rang and he looked up. As he did, a pang of guilt stabbed at him. This was odd. He frequently answered phone calls while he was praying. He didn't usually feel guilty about it, but this time it occurred to him: did he interrupt conversations with people when his phone rang? Not usually. So why would he do it with God? It was Maggie, so he answered her call despite the guilt, hoping she already had news about Daniel.

She didn't.

Damien Foll's lawyer was at the church and wanted to speak with him. Perfect. That was exactly how he wanted to spend the next several minutes of his life. With a sigh, he closed the door to his truck and started the engine, grateful for the air conditioning that would soon cool the cab. He continued to pray as he drove home, until he pulled into the church parking lot to find a new Toyota sedan parked near the door to his parsonage.

He texted Maggie. "Where are you?"

"Church" came back.

"And the lawyer is still there?"

"Yep."

He glanced at the Toyota, wondering why it was parked so far from the church. The lawyer must have started out by knocking on the parsonage door, not realizing that Galen was never home. He grabbed his Walmart bags and headed toward the church.

As he walked up the steps, children spilled out through the door. He stepped to the side to let them pass. Where had they all come from? He didn't recognize any of them. A woman followed behind. He didn't know her either. He smiled and greeted her, but she was in a hurry to catch up to those kids. He turned and tried to count them, but a few of them had already made it to the street. If he had to guess, he thought that woman had seven children.

He made it to the office, eying the suit who stood beside Maggie's desk, despite the two empty chairs nearby. "Did a *giant* family just move in?"

Maggie nodded. "Yes. Six kiddos. We didn't even have a room big enough, but I put some cots in one of the larger ones."

Only six kids. One of them must have been moving fast enough to appear as two children.

Galen could tell the lawyer was feeling impatient and offered his hand. "Galen Turney."

He shook it. "Robert Punzalen. I represent Damien Foll."

Galen nodded his understanding. "It's a pleasure. Would you like to come into my office?" Galen led him in, shut the door behind them, and offered him a seat, which he declined.

"This won't take long. I wanted to speak to you because Damien has decided to plead guilty."

Good for Damien. Galen waited for more.

"And that is a pretty stupid decision. Which he is attributing to you."

Galen suddenly felt very tired. He sat down and leaned back in his chair. "I did not tell him to do anything."

Robert's expression softened. "I understand why, spiritually speaking, you might want to counsel him to plead guilty, but legally speaking, that is a very stupid move. Our whole legal system is designed for people to plead not guilty." He paused to let Galen say something, but he didn't. Robert continued, "If he pleads guilty, I have no room to work for a better sentence." He stepped closer to Galen's desk and lowered his voice. "If he pleads guilty, he's going to get a life sentence. He will die in prison."

Galen didn't know what to say. What did this man want from him? He searched the man's face and found the answer: he wanted Galen to advise Damien to lie. Galen leaned forward and rested his arms on his desk. "I'm happy to go talk with Damien, but I can't tell him to lie. That's not how this works."

Robert's face flooded red and a volley of angry words shot out of his mouth.

Galen rose to his feet, ready to move if necessary. He didn't know what was going to happen, but the lawyer was no longer acting like a lawyer.

"You've ruined this man's life! And for what? A hard line in the religious sand? How ignorant can you be?" He finally turned toward the door.

Galen was speechless. No way this man cared that much about Damien. He must be worried about his record or something. The thought made Galen sick.

Maggie opened the door just in time for Robert to storm through it. She held it open wide and watched him go, and then she looked at Galen. He sank back to his chair, feeling hot and sick. Before he knew she was there, Maggie had wrapped her cool arms around his neck from behind. She kissed him on the temple. "Don't you dare let a single word that man said sink into your heart."

He put a hand on her forearm. "I'm not sure I can stop them."

She spun him around so he could see her. "You haven't ruined anything. And what is a life in prison compared to an eternity of freedom? Let *that* sink in."

He let out a long breath. She was right. Of course. "Thank you." He still felt small, though.

"Just wait till he walks up to you on some street paved with gold. Just wait till Damien Foll thanks you for saving his life."

Chapter 47

Maggie

Maggie's thoughts were racing. That lawyer's visit had done a number on Galen, and she was desperate to make him feel better. There were more people staying at the shelter than usual or expected, and she was trying to figure out how to feed them all. They had food, but not enough, and she wished they hadn't spent so much money on that foolish tent. Although, that tent *had* led to some pretty amazing connections. She supposed she could ask some of those connections for more money. She put her head down on her desk and whispered. "Please, Father, make this simple. Help me to feed these people."

The phone's ring gave her ricocheting thoughts a short reprieve.

"Hello?"

Harry walked into the office at that second and opened his mouth to ask her something. She held up a finger to hold him off. The man on the other end of the line was calling from White Brothers, the largest grocery store chain in the state. One of their stores had just had some sort of ordering mix up and they had a truckload of food with nowhere to go. Her mouth fell open. Could this even be happening? A *truckload?* What next? Giant winged angels were going to carry the food into the church and prepare it?

"So ... could you?"

"I'm sorry," Maggie hurried to say. "Could I what?"

"Could your shelter use the food?" he said slowly.

"Oh, yes! Yes, of course! I was praying for food when you—"

"Terrific," he cut her off. "We'll head toward you now. Will you have people there who can help unload?"

"Definitely! Thank you so much. You're—"

He interrupted her again. "He's about an hour out. You have a good day!"

"You too!"

He hung up and she stared at the phone in her hand until she remembered that Harry was still waiting his turn. She took a deep breath. "What can I do for you, Harry?"

Half his mouth turned up in a sinister smirk that alarmed her. "You can help me pack?" He chuckled, and the chuckle turned into a cough.

She realized then that the weird expression had been Harry's version of a smile. "Pack?" Dare she believe it?

"Yep." He shoved his hands into his pockets and bounced on the balls of his feet.

She was certain she had never seen Harry bounce.

"I got my own place."

She opened her mouth to ask a resounding *how?* but then realized that wouldn't be polite. "Wow, Harry! Congratulations!"

"I can still lead worship, though," he hurried to say.

She bit back a smirk. Harry did play the guitar in the front of the sanctuary, but she'd never really thought of what he did as leading worship.

"I'll still come to church and everything." He laughed again, which turned to hacking again. Once he'd recovered, he said, "Anyway, I wanted to tell you the good news and tell you my room will be opening up soon."

Two zipping thoughts connected in her brain. His room was next door to the one she'd stuffed the big family in. Maybe the mom would let her kids sleep in another room if they were right next door. Then they could all have beds. She tried not to get too excited. Harry had given her false hope before.

"Anyway, I'll be out of here tomorrow."

"Tomorrow?" That was soon. "Will you need help moving?" Most homeless people didn't need help moving out, but Harry had been there so long, he'd amassed quite an estate.

"Sure. Pastor G will help me."

He would? She was certain Galen hadn't promised that. "Does he know your good news yet?"

"No, not yet. I was hoping you could tell him. I think he might be pretty sad to see me go, and I don't want to be there for that." His lip turned up again. "Thought you might do a better job of comforting him in his time of grief."

Someone who didn't know Harry might assume he was being ironic, but she knew that he wasn't. "All right. I'll give him the news."

Harry spun around and left the room. Now Maggie had new thoughts zipping around her brain. How had this come about? Why was he suddenly okay with leaving? And oh how she hoped this one stuck. Her racing mind came back to Daniel then and she thought she should go to the sanctuary to pray so she had a better chance of avoiding further interruptions.

It was dim and quiet and she went to the altar. She knew she could pray anywhere and didn't often go to the altar to do it, but this time it felt appropriate. God had handed her two miracles in the last five minutes and she needed to thank him. She also needed to ask for one more. She'd been asking for Daniel's return for hours, but now she felt more confident.

A God who could get Harry into a home could certainly get Daniel back to his.

She knelt on the worn carpet and leaned her elbows on the altar. She had so much to say that her words refused to organize themselves into sentences she could relay to God. As she often did, she started with gratitude. "Thank you for the truckload of food. I can't even believe that happened. Thank you for Harry's new apartment. Thank you that Galen is being so kind, affectionate, and attentive lately. Thank you for all you're doing here and for the many people who are choosing to know you ..." Before long, without realizing it, she drifted into her wants. "Please make sure we have enough help to unload the truck. Please make sure Harry really goes through with the move and that he stays there. And please, God, please, bring Daniel back to

Harmony. Please don't let anything bad happen to him." Images of all the bad things that could happen to two teenagers on the run flashed through her mind, and her hands started to shake. She clasped them together. "Father," she breathed out, trying to focus. The sanctuary felt so quiet compared to the maelstrom in her head.

"Father," she said again. "I don't know what's going on with Daniel, so I don't exactly know what to ask you for." A wave of guilt hit her then. Why didn't she know what was going on with him? How had she let Harmony and him drift so far away? Her eyes filled with tears. "I'm sorry, God. I'm sorry I didn't do a better job keeping track of Daniel. We're just so busy." A small sob escaped her, and she became self-conscious, though there was no one there to see or hear her.

"We're always so busy." Her words failed her. She was feeling so much, but what should she say? Should she ask God for less busyness? Repent of wanting to walk away? Tell God she didn't want to walk away anymore? Thank God again for all he was doing? Ask him to do even more? Another sob burst out of her, louder this time, and she bowed her head. Hot tears fell onto her folded hands as the thoughts swirled: *please save Daniel; thank you for rescuing my marriage; please tell me how to help Harmony; thank you that Galen didn't die ...* All these things and many more, including thoughts that hadn't even formed yet, tried to come out of her mouth at once and got jammed up.

She snapped her head up and cried out to God, and a torrent of syllables left her mouth. She snapped her mouth shut. What had she just said? She didn't know, but another wave was coming, and she let it out. Jumbled sounds came out, some she was certain she'd never made before, and she felt powerless to stop them. What was happening? Was she losing her mind? If so, she was doing so in the right spot.

She stopped trying to fight it, and the sounds came faster, rising and falling like a language, but it wasn't one she understood. And as this language spilled out of her, her brain stopped spinning. Though she had no idea what she was saying, the things she wanted to say slipped out of her mind and the release of them felt supernaturally sweet.

And then suddenly, she stopped. She hesitated. Was that it? Was it over? As she wondered this, a soft, warm blanket of indescribable peace wrapped around her, and she almost tipped over at the comfort of it. She wanted to curl up right there in front of the altar and go to sleep, and she considered it. She opened her eyes and looked up at the large cross hanging on the wall in front of her, so content she might never have moved if her husband hadn't popped into the sanctuary to ask why a tractor trailer truck was backing up to the church.

Chapter 48

Galen

Harry made it clear that he had no intention of helping to unload the truck, so Galen sent him to round up more help. Then he turned to see Maggie coming toward him.

Galen's breath caught. She looked radiant. He stared at her, trying to figure out why. What had changed? She looked like she always looked, but somehow she looked more *alive*. He went to her and put a hand to each cheek. Then he gave her an enthusiastic kiss.

When he pulled away, she put a hand over her mouth and laughed. "What was *that* for?"

"I don't know," he said and then realizing he sounded like an idiot, "I love you so much."

Her eyes widened in surprise, and this surprise saddened him. Why would it surprise her to hear that? Because he hadn't told her often enough. Because he hadn't *shown* her often enough. He vowed then to make it clear to her every day, so that she'd never again be surprised by a kiss or a declaration of love. But first, they had to unload the groceries. He took her hand in his and turned toward the trailer, where the driver was opening the back doors.

"Does this happen often?" Galen asked, stepping toward the truck.

The man looked at him. "Never in the eight years I've been driving." He looked into the trailer and Galen's eyes followed his.

The White Brothers trailer was chock-full: stacks and stacks of cardboard boxes; shrink-wrapped boxes full of juice bottles; open-topped boxes of produce. Galen stepped closer and the air from the trailer cooled his face. He looked up into the eyes of the ball cap-wearing driver. "We can't thank you enough."

He shrugged. "No need to thank *me*. I go where I'm told. You want some help unloading?" He glanced around. "You probably don't have a pallet jack, huh?"

Galen didn't know exactly what a pallet jack was, but he knew they didn't have one. "No, sorry, but we've got more help coming." He glanced at the door, fervently hoping said help would appear soon.

The driver jumped into the truck as if that weren't an impressive move.

Galen was glad he didn't have to attempt it. "What's your name?"

"Matt." He hefted a box of bagged apples and handed it down to Galen, who took it. Matt was obviously in a hurry to get this done so he could get on with his day.

"Thanks, Matt. Pleasure to meet you." As he turned to carry the apples inside, he saw that Harry had returned with two dozen volunteers. At least, Galen thought they were volunteers. Who knew how Harry had incentivized them?

"Line up!" Harry barked. "Start right here! Form an assembly line all the way to the kitchen!"

"Actually," Galen said, "for now, let's pile it neatly in the sanctuary." He didn't think they'd be able to fit it all in the kitchen and didn't want to have to carry stuff back up the stairs.

Harry was obviously disgusted by Galen usurping his authority, but he didn't argue, and the guests formed something loosely resembling a line while several children weaved around the adults, giggling.

Galen found this sound so refreshing. Over the years, a lot of children had come and gone from Open Door, but there hadn't been an abundance of giggling. Galen handed a box of oranges to his wife. "Careful, this one is wicked heavy."

"Don't insult me," she quipped. Then she leaned in closer. "Where are we going to put all this stuff?"

"I think we're going to have to give some of it away."

She raised an eyebrow as she took a carton of milk off his hands. "Who is going to come to a homeless shelter to take food?"

He shrugged. "Hungry people?"

Box after box went through Galen's hands, and it was a noticeably better assortment than the ones they usually got. Most of their food came from the White Brothers, but these much smaller shipments were usually made up of things that weren't selling or were nearing their expiration dates. So, they got boxes and boxes of gluten-free carrot cake mix and organic kale seasoning, as well as non-fat yogurt and unwashed arugula. He'd always been grateful for these gifts, but this delivery was something different. This one hadn't already been picked over.

He hadn't realized they were winding down until his hands were suddenly empty. He looked out the door to see that the driver was buttoning up the truck, and he went out to thank him again.

"Don't mention it, really." Matt sounded defensive and wouldn't look him in the eye.

"Don't worry, I'm not going to preach to you here in the parking lot."

Matt relaxed a little and almost smiled. "Sorry. I was just preached at in the gas station before I got here, so I didn't want another round. I appreciate you not giving me one."

Galen couldn't *not* ask him to elaborate. "Someone preached to you in the gas station?"

He nodded. "Yep. Told me all about Jesus dying on the cross for my sins." He put his hands on his hips and looked around. "This is a weird town." He reached to open his truck door. "If you'll excuse me, I've got to get going."

"Yes." Galen stepped back. "Of course. Thanks again."

Matt managed a forced smile and then climbed into his truck and closed the door.

Galen waved goodbye, though he thought probably Matt wasn't paying much attention to the rearview mirror, and prayed that he might cross Matt's path again. It wasn't likely. They didn't get a lot of semis in the church parking lot. Usually, Galen took his truck to the store to make a pickup. But God was showing him that anything was possible.

Harry's assembly line was dispersing, and Maggie had vanished. Galen went into the sanctuary to survey their new stock. As he stood there looking down at it all, Maggie appeared behind him and wrapped her arms around his waist.

"I posted on social media. Free food to those in need. We'll see if anyone shows up."

He had a feeling that they might.

Chapter 49

Ruby

Ruby wasn't in the mood to go to a Bible study at a homeless shelter, but her husband was insisting. It had been a long time since she'd seen him so excited about anything. Of course, Open Door and Pastor G had won her over too. She believed in the church's mission and wanted to support it. She just didn't want to go sit in a hard pew on a weeknight. Sunday mornings were one thing. She was fresh in the mornings, and her back didn't hurt nearly as bad in those precious early hours, but by the end of the day, every day, she was in serious pain. Her doctor had told her it was arthritis and given her a prescription, which she hated to take and usually didn't. She preferred massage for pain relief and got one as often as possible. But there was no time for a massage now because her husband had sprung it on her: they were going to church.

On a Friday night.

She touched up her makeup and then went to the garage, where Howard was already waiting in the car. *Oh good grief.* The enormous smile on his face calmed her spirits some. He was ecstatic.

"Buckle up!" he said with an overabundance of cheer.

Grimacing, she did as he said and then endured his humming all the way to church.

The parking lot was full. "What on earth?" she mumbled.

"I know," Howard said. "I wasn't expecting this."

"Are all these people *living* here?" She didn't think they'd be able to find a seat, and they were still ten minutes early.

"I don't think so. Maggie posted online that they had a bunch of free food to give away, and I'm guessing that post got some attention."

Ruby looked at her husband. "People will take food from a homeless shelter?"

He nodded as he put the car in reverse to turn it around. "I guess so." He pulled back out onto the street and drove to the front of the line of cars.

She was annoyed that he hadn't dropped her off at the door first. When he put the two right tires into the ditch, she was beyond annoyed. "How am I supposed to get out? Are you in the mood to rush me to the chiropractor?"

He laughed, and he sounded like a teenager, which further annoyed her. "I'll come around and help you."

She didn't think his help would be sufficient, but they managed, with a dreadful slowness, to get her out of the car and up out of the ditch. But by the time they were crossing the parking lot, the service had started. She could hear those crazy teenagers playing a For King and Country song, and despite her mood, she started to sing along.

They stepped into the sanctuary, and Ruby stopped. Not because there was nowhere to sit, which was the case, but because she was overwhelmed by the feel of the place. She couldn't put her finger on it, but it was almost as though the air itself was buzzing, and a tremendous giddy joy washed over her. She felt like a kid and almost giggled aloud with joy, but at the same time, tears came to her eyes for seemingly no reason. She swatted them away. She wasn't much of a crier, certainly not in public. Howard was looking at her tenderly and she tried to muster up a scolding look. *Don't look at me that way.* But he gave her a broad smile, so she knew something had been lost in translation. He gently tugged her toward the front of the room, which she allowed, even though she'd been a back row Baptist her entire life. They slid into a pew occupied only by Maggie and a petite, plump woman leaning on a walker. This woman didn't acknowledge them, but Maggie's face lit up at the sight of them. She reached to hug Ruby and Ruby stiffened beneath her embrace. One, because having her spine squeezed usually didn't help her pain levels and two, because she hated hugs, but she faked her way through it as she always did and then she turned to face the teenagers up front, who had been joined by an older man playing guitar and a woman on the piano.

They started a new song that Ruby didn't recognize and the lyrics hit her as if they'd been fired by an expert archer: *I see you there beneath your disguise / I see everything you work so hard to hide / But I'm right here waiting to wash it all away / So give me your real heart today.* She grabbed the pew in front of her to steady herself as the waterworks started. No way she was going to avoid crying now. The girl leading the song sang, "Give me your heart," and the rest of the band answered, "I give you my heart, God." The girl repeated the directive, the band repeated the response, and this time the congregation caught on. It sounded like an army behind her, singing, "I give you my heart, God," and though she could barely push her voice out past the lump in her throat, she tried to join them. Over and over, they sang the chorus, and over and over, she sang the words. Of course, she had given her heart to God when she was three, and she'd done it a thousand times since, but right now, she knew she needed to do it again. God's love, his power, was irresistible in this place. He was making himself impossible to ignore, and she didn't want to ignore him.

The chorus changed. The girl sang, "Give me your pain," and everyone answered, "I give you my pain, God." She sang it again, and the congregation responded with more zeal. As Ruby sang the words, she was thinking about emotional pain, concentrating on giving God her emotional hurt, but as she repeated the words, she felt a weird tingling in her lower back. She shifted her weight to try to make it go away, but it grew stronger. Scared that something was really wrong, she sat down, still holding on to the pew in front of her. Maggie on one side of her and her husband on the other both turned to ask her if she was okay.

She didn't know the answer to their question. The tingling stopped, but she was still shaken by it. What was wrong with her? She'd never felt that feeling before. Then she realized that the pain was gone. She gasped. Wait. For real? She stood on shaky legs and shifted her weight around, trying to make the pain come back, trying to dismiss the foolish hope she was feeling.

But the pain didn't come back.

A broad smile took over her face as she turned it toward heaven. Howard asked her again if she was all right, and she ignored him. She was too busy thanking God.

The song faded to a close and Pastor Galen went to the front of the sanctuary, but he didn't step up onto the platform. He thanked Blanktified and friends for their service and then he held his arms out to his sides. "Look, everyone. Look what God is doing!" The place erupted in cheers. Under normal circumstances, such a show of enthusiasm would have made her distinctly uncomfortable, but Ruby didn't mind so much tonight.

Galen waited for everyone to settle down and then spoke softly into the microphone. "If

I'd known free food would bring you all here, we would have started giving it out long ago." A ripple of laughter went through the room. "But seriously, thank you all for coming and thank you to those of you who stuck around after you filled up your trunks. The Bible tells us that there is power in our testimony, in our stories of what God has done. I know there are people here with miraculous stories. Would any of you like to share?"

Ruby grew hot. She could feel every eye on her. She checked in with her back. Yup, still pain free. But that didn't mean she'd had a miracle, and she certainly wasn't going to speak into a microphone in front of all these people. She intensely studied the floor until she realized that both Maggie and Howard were turned toward the back of the room. Oh good, someone else was going to do it. Thank God. She turned to look as well and saw Galen handing the microphone to a woman in one of those coveted back row seats.

"Hi," she said, her voice shaky with nerves. "My name is Christine. My family and I go to church at First Baptist, and we've known Jesus forever." She tittered. "We came here tonight for the food—"

She was interrupted by laughter, and she smiled down at the two kids beside her, the older of which looked mightily embarrassed. "But we stayed for the service, and I'm so glad we did." She got choked up and paused to rein it in. Ruby could relate to the feeling. She tried again, "It's hard to explain what just happened, and you guys are gonna think I'm nuts, but I've had terrible jaw pain for months now. It wraps around my head and neck and makes life miserable. I take medication, which helps some, but it hasn't cured it. So my doctor scheduled me for a steroid shot on Monday." She rubbed at her jaw with two fingers. "But I don't need to go now. While we were singing, the jaw pain disappeared."

Ruby's eyes snapped back to her feet.

"And I can't explain it, but I know that it won't come back."

There was a rustling that Ruby attributed to the handing off of the microphone and then a man was speaking. She had trouble focusing on what he was saying, though, as she was wrestling with the Holy Spirit, who was clearly telling her to share her miracle as well.

I can't.

I'll help you.

I can't.

I want you to.

I can't. Ruby bit her lip so hard it hurt. *God, please don't make me.*

The urge passed and Ruby let out a long breath. God had let her off the hook. She checked in with her back again. Had he taken away his healing as punishment? No, he had not.

Galen returned to the front of the room, shared the Gospel message with a simple eloquence she admired, and then gave an altar call. So many people flooded to the altar that there was nowhere to kneel. She grew impatient. She wanted to take her healing and quietly go home, but no one else was in a hurry. Everyone else was praying. So it was either sit there and sulk or join in. She opted for the latter, thanking God for a healing that she didn't completely trust yet.

Chapter 50

Daniel

Daniel woke up with his back against a tree and Ember leaning on his arm, which had lost all feeling. He looked down at her and decided he wouldn't move yet, no matter how uncomfortable he was. He wasn't supposed to have fallen asleep anyway. She'd been too scared to sleep in the woods, so he'd promised he would stay awake and stand watch, which he had done, for the first few hours. They'd spent the first night in a park, and he didn't understand how that was safer than where they were now, but she'd been more comfortable there.

They were covered up in a light coat, but his back and butt were cold and damp. This hadn't been the best idea, but they'd survived the night, and he was confident they could make it to Mattawooptock by nightfall, even if they didn't catch another ride.

Hitchhiking had proved harder than he'd thought it would be. Each time a vehicle didn't pick them up, a small voice suggested to Daniel that God was protecting them from that vehicle, but Daniel told himself that no one was picking them up because there were two of them. Two straggly looking teenagers posed more of a threat than either would on their own, but he certainly wasn't going to split up, especially not with the state Ember was in.

If he'd known she would have struggled so much with this trip, he might never have started it. There were moments when he'd really regretted it, but then he'd asked himself, what other choice did he have? He looked down at her pale face and listened to her soft breathing. He'd managed to get them food, but not much, and it hadn't been healthy. Now he was out of money.

She stirred and he looked away, not wanting to get caught staring at her. Thirty seconds passed and she pulled herself off him. He leaned forward immediately, his body screaming for a change of position. "Sorry," she mumbled. "Didn't mean to make you into a bed."

"No worries." He tried to play it cool, but he'd really enjoyed being her bed.

She stretched, and he allowed himself to look at her. "I'm freezing."

He waited a beat before answering, trying to be patient. All she had done since they'd left Portland was complain. "We'll warm up once we start walking." He pulled his feet under himself. "Which, we should do soon.

Whenever you're ready." He rose to his feet and looked down at her.

"I have to pee."

"Yeah, me too. Go ahead. I won't look."

She tipped her head to the side and glared at him. "I don't want to go in the woods."

He looked in the direction of the road, which he couldn't quite see. "Then we'd better start walking. Give me just a second." He stepped past her, went fifty feet away and took care of business. Then he returned to her, feeling a little embarrassed. She had gotten to her feet and was holding his jacket out to him.

"Do you want to wear it?"

She shook her head. "I'm fine."

He put it on, felt how damp it was, and took it back off. "Let's go, then." He started toward the road.

She groaned again and followed.

He swung one leg over the guardrail and then turned to help her over it, but she declined his hand and managed it herself. Two cars zipped by, one in each direction, their wind blowing invisible dirt into Daniel's cheek. He tried to wipe it away. "You want to try for a ride or do you want to walk for a while?"

"Neither," she snapped. "But I really need to pee. Where's the nearest store?"

How should he know? Did she think he had a maps app in his head? They'd both turned off their phones because they didn't want their mothers to track them. He wasn't even sure where they were, but he was sure they were close to Augusta. They'd stayed off the highways, and not knowing many town names or any route names, Daniel had focused on heading northeast. He hadn't told her this, but the ride they'd hitched on Route 1 had taken them a little *too* east, so last night, they'd started heading due north. She hadn't seemed to notice. She didn't seem to be aware of anything except putting one foot in front of the other. While it made him feel good to have her relying on him, it also scared him.

By sheer luck, they'd run into the Kennebec River, which also ran through Mattawooptock. His plan was to follow the river, even if it didn't take him in a straight line. This plan made him feel smart, but he still didn't know what town they were in or where the next bathroom was. She was still looking at him, waiting for an answer. "I'll let you know when I see it, but we've got to be getting close to Augusta, and there are a million bathrooms there."

She groaned. "Can we just stay there when we get there?"

He snickered humorlessly. "What? What would that accomplish?"

"I don't know," she whined, "but I don't want to walk anymore. I don't feel good, I'm dizzy, and my feet hurt so bad."

He was sure that they did. His feet were killing him, and he had way better shoes than she did. It occurred to him to steal her some new shoes, but he wasn't confident that he wouldn't get caught. An encounter with the police would certainly slow them down, and the closer he grew to Open Door Church, the more desperate he was to get there. "I'm sure we'll find a ride in Augusta."

"Okay, fine!" she snapped and turned off the road and headed into the woods. He stopped and waited for her, and then they continued walking, without conversation. They came to a church with a car in the lot, and Daniel considered stopping to ask for help, but he didn't quite dare. He didn't want to be judged, didn't know if they'd help, and didn't want to deal with rejection.

Seeming to read his mind, Ember asked for the tenth time, "Can't you call these people and ask them to come get us?"

"No." He didn't want to turn his phone on, and he wasn't going to call Galen after all this time and act like nothing had changed.

Lots had changed.

"I don't know why you think we can show up and they'll help us. But they won't help us enough to come get us?"

They'd already had this argument. "I don't even know who works there now. I don't know who to call." It was far more complicated than this, but he didn't understand it himself, so how could he explain it to her? He heard a car coming from behind. "You ready to try for a ride?"

"Yes," she said quickly.

He kept walking, but he turned to face the oncoming car and stuck his thumb out. It turned out to be a decrepit minivan, and wonder of all wonders, it slowed to a stop.

"Please sit in the back with me," she said quietly, her voice laced with fear.

Chapter 51

Ember

Daniel took Ember's hand and gently pulled her toward the driver's side window.

"Where you headed?" a scruffy man asked around the cigarette hanging out of his mouth.

"North," Daniel said. "Mattawooptock, eventually."

Ember did not have a good feeling about this and gave Daniel's hand a death grip. She did not want to get into that van.

"Matta*what*? Where's that?"

"North," Daniel said again.

The man grinned, still gripping the cigarette between dry, flaky lips. He looked Ember up and down with cloudy eyes that made her skin crawl. "Climb in, then." He tipped his head toward the other side of the van.

Daniel led her around the back of the van, even though it would have been quicker to go around the front. Was he afraid the man would run them over? At the back of the van, she stopped. "I don't want to, Daniel," she whispered.

He yanked on her, obviously frustrated. "Come on, before he changes his mind."

She let herself be pulled, but kept protesting. "Please, I don't like this guy."

"I don't either, but he's going to give us a ride." He reached the sliding door and reached for the handle. "It'll be okay. I won't let anything happen to you." He slid the door open.

Half of her believed him; the other half of her knew he was only a kid. Daniel motioned for her to climb in, but when she hesitated, he went in first. Then he stopped, bent over, with his butt near her face. What was wrong? Why had he stopped? He backed up and then climbed into the backseat before reaching back for her hand. She stepped up into the van and as soon as her eyes adjusted to the lack of light, she saw his conundrum. A baby in a car seat sat in the middle seat, and a pit bull sat in the back. Oh boy. This was awesome. She wanted to sit beside Daniel, make him snuggle up to the pit bull, but she didn't. She settled instead beside the sleeping baby, whose head was surrounded by a cloud of smoke.

"You gonna shut the door?" the man croaked.

"Sorry, yes," she stammered and slid the door shut. Then she tried not to breathe. The van smelled like rotten garbage.

Daniel put his hand on her shoulder and gave her a little squeeze. Tears sprang to her eyes. How had her life come to this? She wished she were dead. She wished she'd never left Portland.

"What's in Mattawooptock?" the man hollered at the rearview.

"Family," Daniel called back. She didn't know if he was lying or if he really considered those church people his family. She couldn't believe that she was working so hard to go get rescued by a bunch of religious freaks. She couldn't imagine what they were going to do to help, but Daniel swore up and down that they would know what to do, and who else did she have to listen to besides Daniel?

She could only hold her breath for so long and considered pulling her shirt up over her nose, but didn't want to offend the driver. She tried breathing through her mouth. That was worse. She went back to not breathing.

"How far are you going?" Daniel asked.

The man laughed, a throaty, threatening laugh. "Not sure yet."

She'd been scared before, many times, but maybe not this scared. She wanted to die, yes, but not at the hands of this lunatic in this disgusting van. She glanced at the baby. Was she even breathing? Her little lips were moving almost imperceptibly as she sucked on a faded pacifier. So yes, she was alive. "What's the baby's name?" she asked without meaning to.

"Camilla," the man said cheerfully. "You like babies?"

What kind of a question was that? "Sure."

They rode in silence for a while until Daniel whispered, "This is Augusta." He sounded so encouraged by this. She wished the town had the same effect on her. She didn't know exactly where Mattawooptock was, but she knew it was still a long ways from Augusta. At least there was more to look at now, something other than river and trees, and she tried to be entertained by what she saw out her window, her mouth watering when they went by a Dunkin. Then the signs of city began to fade and the trees became more prevalent again.

The pit bull barked, and Ember jumped in her seat. His barking got louder until she thought her head was going to explode, but then he stopped as suddenly as he began. "He always gets shook up when he sees another dog," the driver explained. The baby's eyes were open and wide now and Ember wished she could steal her away from this man. The thought surprised her. What made her think the baby would be any better off with her? At least this guy had a car, and he could afford gas and cigarettes. He slowed for a yellow light and then took a sharp left before the light turned red.

"Where are you headed?" Daniel asked, and Ember heard concern in his voice. "I don't want to get too far away from the river."

The man laughed again, and the hair on the back of her neck stood up. "Don't worry. You want to get to Mattawooptock, don't you?" They were back in pure forest now, and Ember couldn't see any road signs.

She felt Daniel's breath on her ear. "Get ready to jump out if he stops."

What? How exactly was that going to work? She wouldn't even be able to get the door open! Her heart raced and she fought against hysteria. She might want to die, but she didn't want to get Daniel killed. If he thought their best option was to try to jump out of a minivan, then that's what she would try to do.

"We're going south," Daniel whispered. "Next stop sign or light—"

"What're you guys whisperin' about back there?" He looked in his rearview again.

Ember was so glad she hadn't buckled up, and hoped Daniel hadn't either. She heard Daniel's phone chime as he turned it on. Good. That was smart. "Nothing!" he said, trying to sound light. Ember wondered if he'd tried to cover up the phone's noise with his voice. If so, he'd been a little late.

The man lit another cigarette, and it seemed that he gave the van some more gas. The baby spit out her pacifier and started to cry. The man swore. Ember reached over to put the pacifier back in her mouth, but the man yelled at her, "Don't touch the kid!"

She yanked her hand back, trembling. *Never mind the baby, Ember. Focus on getting that door open.*

Finally, the van slowed and Ember felt Daniel lean forward. She looked through the windshield. They were coming to a light at an intersection. The driver looked in the rearview. She thought about reaching for the door. When should she do it? They had slowed down, but not enough, and they were fast approaching the intersection. Was he going to blow through it without stopping? There were several cars in the junction, and he had a red light. No, he wasn't going to stop. That much was clear. She braced herself for the collision that would most certainly hit her as he crossed against oncoming traffic. Better her than the baby. But then, at the last second, he slammed on the brakes, throwing them all forward.

Before she knew what was happening, Daniel had reached past her and ripped the door open and was pulling her out of the van. One leg hit the ground and then she was falling, but Daniel had her hand and he kept pulling until she was in the ditch, with her feet under her. She reached for him with her other hand and buried her face in his chest, sobbing.

"It's okay, it's okay. He's driving away."

She let him hold her and kept crying. She didn't think she could survive this world much longer, even with Daniel's help.

Chapter 52

Maggie

Saturday night at Open Door Church brought guest speaker Kevin McLaughlin. It was obvious that Galen was happy to have a break. He'd spent all day getting Harry moved, which was certainly a joyous occasion, but Maggie knew that the trouble with Daniel was weighing heavily on her husband. She'd been texting Harmony every few hours for updates, but there were none. She'd manipulated Harmony into sending her a recent photo of Daniel, which Galen had then forwarded to the Portland Police.

Most of the members of Blanktified weren't able to attend that night, so they only had lead singer Todd, who was doing his best to lead worship to a packed house. Though they'd given out no food that day, at six o'clock, people had flooded through the door. Maggie couldn't believe it. There wasn't an open seat in the house. In fact, the big family with six kids, all of whom had gone to the altar the night before, had settled onto the floor in front of the first pew. Maggie loved seeing so many kids in the church. It reminded her of the days when a young Daniel, a young Isaiah, and a young Elijah had enjoyed their run of the place.

Now, her boys were teenagers. She couldn't believe it. Where had the time gone? And so was Daniel. He'd looked so different in that photo. So old. So tough. What had Portland done to him? She wished he'd never left them.

Kevin welcomed them all and then prayed over them. After saying "amen," he stood with one hand on the music stand in front of him, where he'd set his Bible, and stared out at the congregation. There was a long, awkward wait, and Maggie marveled at how quiet and patient the guests were being. Maybe all the extra visitors were motivating them to be on their best behavior.

Finally, he said, "Folks, I'm so glad to see so many new faces. I can't tell you how it tickles me. And I'm wondering, did you know that God is running a homeless shelter here?"

Many people laughed, but Maggie didn't know if Kevin had been trying to be funny. He didn't smile.

"God has done so much with this place," Kevin said, "and I think he's only getting started. So my question is, who here wants to be a part of it?"

Maggie's breath caught. What was he doing?

No one responded, and he rephrased his invitation. "I'm asking, who wants to roll up their sleeves and help this place? We need people to teach, we need people to clean, to cook, to work in the office ..." He kept talking as Maggie frantically tried to think of a way to stop him. They'd learned over the years that it *really* wasn't a good idea to ask visitors to get to work right away. Or ever. Asking people to work usually sent them packing.

Not this time. This time hands were popping up all over the sanctuary.

"Maggie, do you have a notepad and a pen?" He was staring at her, waiting for her to move, which she finally did.

She hopped up and headed toward the office, but Kim stopped her by holding out the attendance clipboard. Yes, of course, that would work. "Thank you," she mouthed to the guest who had been in charge of attendance for over a year. If Open Door didn't take attendance at Bible study, guests tended to skip Bible study. She ripped off the top sheet of paper, shoved it into her pocket, and returned to Kevin with her gift outstretched.

He pointed toward the front row. "Start right there. Everybody, if you want to be a part of this awesome move of God, write your name, a phone number, and how you've been equipped to serve. If you don't know how you're equipped, don't worry about it. God will make it clear. You can just leave that part blank."

She stood in the front of the church with her mouth open, watching people she didn't know write their names down. This was incredible. She would actually get to make up a schedule for people. Never had a clerical task sounded like so much fun. She floated back to her seat.

As the clipboard circulated, Kevin started teaching about the Comforter, who was a gift from Jesus. Except for the rustling of children, the place was silent. He had their attention.

Galen came in late and squished himself into the pew beside her. She slid over until the woman beside her gave her a dirty look. She tried to smile at her, but the woman had already turned back to Kevin.

"Now, I hear we had a healing here last night!" Kevin said with triumph in his voice.

A few people cheered.

"How would you like to have a few more?"

They cheered again.

"The Bible calls for the leaders of the church to lay hands on the sick. Pastor Galen, would you come join me?"

Looking hesitant, Galen stood.

"And it tells us to anoint them with oil in the name of the Lord. God doesn't want you to suffer. He wants to set you free. If you need prayer for healing, please come on down here and we will ask God to heal you!" He had such a commanding voice for such an elderly man. Maggie loved the sound of it.

At first, no one moved. Kevin handed a vial of oil to Galen, who looked at it uncomfortably. They'd never done this before. They'd prayed for healings and had witnessed them, especially when Daniel had been around, but they'd never used oil. Still, it was in the Bible, so Maggie prayed that God would guide Galen in how to do this.

Roger, one of their long-time guests, was the first to stand. Roger used a cane, and Maggie knew that he had at least one bad hip, if not two. Maggie was glad to see him stop in front of Kevin, so Galen could watch Kevin at work and see how on earth he was supposed to do this. But it turned out not to be complicated. Kevin dabbed a bit of oil on Roger's head with his thumb and then he bowed his head and spoke too softly for Maggie to hear. As he prayed, a woman Maggie didn't know went to stand in front of Galen, tears streaming down her face. Galen did as Kevin had done and began to pray.

Despite the lines growing long, Kevin took his time praying for Roger, and when he finished, Roger headed back to his seat. Maggie watched him come. Halfway to his pew, he stopped. Then he picked up his cane, stood still for a few seconds, and then returned to his seat without limping. When he got to his pew, he let out a little yelp of excitement and the people sitting nearby clustered around him to ask questions.

Then the woman Galen had prayed for cried out, "I can hear!" and the people around her started clapping and whooping it up.

And the lines kept growing.

Chapter 53

Maggie

Maggie got to church early on Sunday to find Blanktified rehearsing and about thirty people already in the sanctuary singing along. She hoped the young band didn't mind. She hurried to turn on the air conditioning and then ran around picking up trash and treasures left behind the night before. That service had gone on till nine o'clock, with a total of twelve people receiving healing for various ailments. Maggie still couldn't wrap her head around it. Voices in her head said things like, "They got caught up in the moment and imagined it" and "They're faking it for attention" but she tried to ignore these voices, tried to believe what the Bible told her to be true. God had healed people all the time back then. Why wouldn't he do so now?

Someone tapped her on the shoulder and she turned to see Phyllis, the owner of Curl Up and Dye. Maggie let out a little squeal and gave her a big hug. "What are you doing here?"

Phyllis laughed and held up a hand, using her other one to adjust the thick purse strap on her shoulder. "Don't worry, I'm not leaving my church or anything, but my nephew ..." Her eyes scanned the front to locate him, and then she pointed. "You know, Todd, he's my nephew ..." She turned her eyes back to Maggie and her voice grew sober. "He's been telling me about what's been going on here. The people getting saved? The healings? And then I saw you guys in the paper, and I just had to come see for myself!"

Uh-oh. "The paper?"

"Why, yes! I mean, you guys are in the paper all the time, but this morning was different. Front page headline said something like—she held her hands up as if she were envisioning a marquee—'Apparent Revival Among The Homeless: Healings Abound!'" She dropped her hands and looked at Maggie expectantly.

Maggie was speechless. They'd published that?

"Todd told me that it's all true! It's crazy!"

Maggie laughed. "Yes, it is. Well, welcome. I'm glad you're visiting. And you'll get to hear Blanktified!"

She shook her head. "I've heard them play *plenty.*"

Maggie inferred that she was dissing them a little, and Maggie felt defensive.

"But I'm glad I'm visiting too. I'd like to get a little of what you've got here and take it back to my church."

Maggie assumed she didn't mean the homeless people. "Great!"

"Yes, so tell me. How did you do it?"

Maggie looked around her sanctuary as if the answer lay there somewhere. "I don't know. I mean, we didn't. We asked God to help us, and he did it. He did it all."

"So cool. So, where do you sit?"

Maggie took her to her spot. "Usually somewhere right here. If you want to save me a seat, I've got to run around a little."

Phyllis winked at her. "Of course."

Maggie went to the office to check for messages. She sat down at her desk and turned on her computer. As she waited for it to boot up, people continued to stream into the sanctuary. There were messages, lots of them, more than Maggie had time to deal with. She scanned subject lines for emergency language, didn't see any, and then stuck her head into Galen's office. She started a little when she found him on his knees. "You okay?"

He looked up. "Definitely." He pulled himself to his feet. "There are a lot of people out there. I thought I could use some help."

She went to him and gave him a long hug. "You've got it." She stepped back and smiled up at him. "*You* are obviously God's favorite."

He laughed, his eyes sparkling. He gave her a kiss. "So are you. And you're my favorite too."

She pulled away, regretfully. "I want to get in there, or I won't get a seat."

Sure enough, the seating was tight. Someone had lined folding chairs up along the back wall, and these were filling up too. Maggie climbed over a few people to squeeze in beside Phyllis.

"This is incredible," Phyllis said. "I've never seen anything like it." She looked at Maggie. "Is your salon getting busier too?"

Maggie laughed. "Actually, no. I'm doing a lot for the guests, the people staying here, but I haven't gotten a lot of outside traffic." For once, she was grateful for this. She had enough going on.

"Well, maybe I could come in once in a while and give you a break."

Maggie turned toward her, not trying to hide her surprise. "Phyllis! I love you!"

Phyllis leaned and bumped her shoulder against Maggie's, laughing. "I love you too."

Galen walked in and headed for the front, and Blanktified invited everyone to stand and join them in praise. As Maggie stood to accept their invitation, she turned to put her Bible on her seat, and that's when she saw who had just walked in.

Two teens, looking haggard and bruised. A girl with pink hair holding a young man's hand.

Daniel.

Chapter 54

Daniel

Daniel stepped into the sanctuary and stopped. His brain registered that the place was packed, but this was not what stopped him. He stopped because he suddenly felt as though he was underwater, in very warm water, and he couldn't breathe. His brain told his mouth to open, told his lungs to inhale, and, as if they were entities separate from himself, he felt them obey. He sucked in a lungful and he heard a rushing wind, so loud it scared him. He looked around for the source of the wind, but there was nothing to see. No people bracing against the wind, no hymnals getting blown across the room, no roof getting ripped off. Still, he heard the wind. He caught his breath. The feeling of the warm water didn't leave him, but he could breathe now. He knew Ember was looking up at him expectantly, but she seemed very far away.

Maggie's squeal startled him out of his head, and she came rushing toward him, stumbling over someone's foot and almost falling before finding her footing and running to him. She wrapped her arms around him, and he burst into tears. He let go of Ember to return the hug, and he let himself cry. He was twelve years old again, safe with rock-steady Maggie, who loved him like a son. The music continued and the congregation started to sing, but still they stood there. Though he was in the very back of the room, he could hear voices behind him singing. Beautiful, ethereal voices hitting every note perfectly.

A strong hand fell on Daniel's shoulder, and he looked up to see Galen, his eyes full of love and concern. This made him cry even harder, but he didn't care. He didn't care if he cried for the rest of his life. He didn't care who saw. He was so relieved to be there, to be safe, to be loved.

Maggie stepped back to make room for Galen to hug him, which Galen did. "Welcome home, son," he said into his ear, and Daniel thought he might never stop crying.

Galen let go of him and held him at arm's length.

Remembering Ember, Daniel reached out with one arm and drew her toward them. "We need your help."

Galen nodded. "And you've got it." He glanced back over his shoulder, toward the front. "I'm supposed to teach soon. Do you want me to find someone to fill in for me?"

Daniel shook his head quickly. "No, it can wait."

Galen nodded, gave his arm another squeeze, and returned to the front of the room.

"Can I let your mom know you're here?" Maggie asked.

Daniel couldn't believe she'd asked his permission. "Yes, but ..." He glanced at Ember, then back to Maggie. "It's complicated," he said over the music. "I don't want Ember's mom to know where she is. And could she get something to eat and drink?" He hesitated and then explained, "She's pregnant."

Ember gave him an incredulous look, but Daniel ignored it. They were past pretense.

"Of course!" Maggie exclaimed, without an ounce of judgment in her voice. "Let's go downstairs." She led them down into the basement and Daniel was sad to leave the sanctuary, but he needed to take care of Ember.

They sat down at a table, and Ember put her head down on her arms. He rubbed her back as he explained to Maggie, "She's exhausted. She doesn't feel well, I guess because she's pregnant, and we haven't eaten in more than twenty-four hours. We walked most of the way." He took a breath. "Should have walked the rest," he added, and Maggie didn't ask him to explain. She set two glasses of water on the table. "I'll get some sandwiches together in a jiffy, but I really want to tell your mom you're okay. How can we do that without alerting Ember's mother?"

He sighed. His mother's needs were the last thing on his mind. "I'll do it." He took his phone out of his back pocket and turned it on.

"What are you doing?" Ember cried accusingly.

"Don't worry," he said for the millionth time, "we're safe now."

His mother answered, and despite his anger, it felt really good to hear her voice.

"Don't freak out—"

She immediately freaked out.

"Mom, stop! My phone's going to die."

"Why haven't you called? I've left you a thousand messages!"

"I haven't listened to my messages because there were a thousand of them! Please stop freaking out!"

She calmed down a little. "Where are you?"

"Mom, this is serious. You *can't* tell Ember's mom where we are, but we're at church. We're with Maggie."

297

"What? Why? What are you doing there?"

"I'll explain later," he said, hoping he would never have to. "But we're fine. I'll call you later." She was still talking, but he hung up.

Maggie set two sandwiches in front of them and then sat across from them. "When you're ready, tell me what you need."

Ember started on her sandwich, and Daniel started talking. He told Maggie everything.

Chapter 55

Galen

Galen waited for the corrections officer to open the door so he could see Damien. They were ten minutes late, and Galen worried that something was wrong, but finally, a man wearing at least fifty pounds of gear around his waist appeared to unlock the door for him.

Galen needn't have worried. Nothing appeared to be wrong with Damien—he looked like a new man. "How are you doing?" Galen asked, after the robot reminded them the call would be recorded.

"So good. You won't even believe it."

"Oh, I've come to believe a lot of unbelievable things lately. Try me."

Damien grinned. "They've got a Bible study in here, and I went to it, and I told them about everything that has happened to me, and about me following Jesus. By the way, I can't even explain how *real* he feels to me right now, man. I read my Bible all the time, and it's like he's right there in the cell with me. I mean, jail still sucks, and it probably always will, but I don't feel alone, and I don't feel scared. It's so weird."

Galen nodded, not wanting to interrupt.

"Anyway, after I finished my story, a few other guys wanted to get saved and so they did, right there in that Bible study, and then the next Bible study, even more guys came, and they wanted to get saved too. It's spreading through this place like wildfire. The pastor who does the Bible study ran out of Bibles. I thought about letting one of the guys borrow mine, but I didn't." He laughed. "Didn't want to. Anyway, he said he was going to get more, but he has to have them shipped here. He's not allowed to bring them in."

It was obvious Damien wanted Galen to talk now, but he wasn't sure what to say. "That sounds awesome, Damien. Something similar is happening at the shelter right now, lots of new people coming in, lots of people getting saved, lots of miracles—"

Damien slapped the small table in front of him. "I knew it!"

What had he known, exactly?

"I knew things were going to happen at the shelter. I've been praying for you guys, for all of you, especially for my friends."

Galen couldn't remember Damien having any friends at the shelter, but he saw no need to share that. "Harry even moved out!"

Damien laughed. "Hosanna! See! Now, *that's* a miracle!"

Galen joined him in his laughter, mostly because he'd shouted *hosanna* into the phone.

Damien grew serious all of a sudden. "I'm telling *everyone*, Pastor G. I mean, not everyone listens because some people hate me for what I did, and they don't want to hear anything outta me, and I don't blame them. And a few guys act like I'm some kind of hero, but I tell them it ain't like that, not at all. I did the worst thing in the world, and I'll never stop being sorry. But I'm going to try to make the best of it by trying to tell everyone in here and everyone in the next place about Jesus."

Galen was speechless again. "That's so wonderful, Damien. I'll be praying for you."

"And I'll be praying for you too. You'll keep coming to see me? They'll be moving me soon." He choked up on the last few words.

"Yeah, yeah, of course, Damien. As long as I'm able to, I'll keep coming to see you."

"Because you know"—his eyes were wet now—"I'm going to be in here, and eventually in the prison, for the rest of my life. That's a long time."

Galen nodded. "I know." He searched for the right words. "I was so impressed when I heard that you had told the truth. That took a lot of guts, Damien."

Damien nodded and swallowed. "I figured it was the least I could do. I can never make up for what I did, and I didn't deserve forgiveness." His voice was almost inaudible.

Wanting to bring him back to his previous joy, Galen said, "You didn't deserve it, but you have it. You're going to do a lot of good, Damien. I know it."

He gave Galen an earnest look. "I know it too. And I know I've got help. Sometimes I can almost hear it buzzing. It's like there's this power in the air."

Epilogue

One Year Later

Daniel stepped up to the front and laid his open, well-worn Bible on the music stand. He looked out at the open house and cleared his throat. It didn't matter how many times he led Bible study, it still made him a nervous wreck to do so.

He took a steadying breath. "It's cool to see so many new faces out there tonight. Welcome to Open Door. For those of you who don't know me, my name is Daniel Holland. Yes, I am only seventeen, and I appreciate the opportunity to be up here in front of you. I don't take it lightly, and don't worry, I'm not going to preach to you. But I am so unbelievably excited about Jesus and about his Word that Pastor G lets me share what God has been showing me. So please excuse my age.

"I literally grew up in this shelter. My mom"—he flashed a loving smile at his mother, who was sitting in the front row—"brought me home from the hospital to this church, and I spent the first twelve years of my life here. I went away for a while, and I'm so grateful to be back. So, when I welcome you to Open Door, I'm really welcoming you to my home.

"Now"—he clapped his hands together—"for those of you who *do* know me, I thank you for giving me the respect you would give an adult, and I ask you tonight to give that same respect to my dearest friend, Ember. God has told her to share her testimony with you tonight, and though she's not excited about doing that"—he grinned at her—"she is being obedient. She is also only seventeen, but she has been through more in her life than most people, and I think you'll be blessed by what she has to say. I'd like to introduce her with one of my favorite verses." He looked at his Bible, even though he didn't need to.

"In the first chapter of Jeremiah, God said to a young Jeremiah, 'Before I formed you in the womb I knew you, And before you were born I consecrated you.'" He looked up. "Now, he's talking to Jeremiah here, but this shows us that he chooses us and sets us apart before we are even born. And then Jeremiah said to God, 'I do not know how to speak, Because I am a youth.' And God answered, 'Do not say, "I am a youth," Because everywhere I send you, you shall go, And all that I command you,

you shall speak. Do not be afraid of them, For I am with you to deliver you.'"

He paused. "God chose Ember before she was born to speak to you today. He has already done amazing things through her, and I know he will continue to do amazing things, no matter what her age. So when she speaks to you, know that what she's saying is true and it's from God." He nodded to Ember, who was sitting beside Harmony. She stood and came to the front as he scooped up his Bible and got out of her way. He gave her hand a squeeze as she turned to face her audience.

The room was completely silent.

"I am so scared right now," she said, and several people laughed.

Someone called out, "You're okay. You've got this."

"My story is a little crazy. I hate telling it because it's so sad and disturbing, but God has told me to share it because there are lots of sad and disturbing stories in this world, and he wants you to know that he is in the business of rescuing people from sad and disturbing stories."

She took a deep breath and looked at Daniel, who nodded and smiled, wishing he could make her more aware of the strength within her. "I grew up in Portland, and from a very young age, I was abused by my uncle. It started so young that I didn't really understand what was happening or how wrong it was. I was ashamed, but it was almost like I couldn't process what was happening and why I was ashamed. I started using when I was very young because that made me feel better. It made me feel good enough that I was almost okay, but when I wasn't high or drunk, I was often suicidal." She paused for so long that Daniel wondered if she would continue.

"Anyway, Daniel was my first real friend, the first person I trusted. At the time, I didn't know why he was different, but now I know it was God. And then I got pregnant, and I didn't know what to do. I was only sixteen, and my mother wanted me to have an abortion. When I'd told her about what her brother was doing to me, she didn't believe me, but when I told her I was pregnant, she immediately knew who the father was. I didn't think of abortion as being wrong necessarily, not when other people did it, but I really didn't want to do it. I didn't want to be a mother, wasn't ready to be a mother, and was scared out of my mind. Again, I wanted to die.

"But Daniel wouldn't let that happen, and he brought me here." She smiled at him. "The trip almost killed us, I'm not even kidding. We walked most of the way, slept in the woods, and almost got kidnapped by some psycho in a minivan."

Laughter swept through the room, but they soon quieted. They didn't want to miss anything.

"But we got here, and I felt real love for the first time in my life. I'd felt it from Daniel, but here I was surrounded by it, and it was impossible to ignore. I hated this place at first, thought everyone was crazy with all the religious talk … and I still think they're a little crazy …" She paused to let them laugh. "But now I know that what they say and what they believe is true. There is no way God isn't real because my heart could never have healed on its own." She got choked up then, and Daniel thought about going up there with her for support, but he held back.

She drew a shaky breath and kept going. "Pastor G and Maggie helped me to find an awesome couple to adopt my baby, and they will give him a loving home where he will grow up knowing God, and he never has to know the terrible way he came to be. All he will know is that he is loved." The tears came in force, and Maggie grabbed a handful of tissues and pushed them into her hand. Daniel went to her too and put his hand on her back. "My mother swore he would be messed up, saying he'd die at birth, but she was wrong. He is perfectly healthy."

She took another long breath and looked out at her audience. "There was so much death, so much hatred in my heart, and it's all gone. I still hurt sometimes because of what I've been through, but I ask God for comfort and he gives it." She smiled up at Daniel. "I can't tell you what it's done for me to know people like Daniel, Isaiah, and Elijah. I know they are young, but these guys are heroes for God. They live with fire in their veins, and every day I ask God to give me more of what they've got." She wiped at her eyes and nose. "I'm not telling you to worship them, but if you have any questions or you want to hear stories about how real God is, these guys know, and they'll tell you, and they'll help you. No matter what you need, they'll help you. I'm so grateful for them." She flashed a smile at the sound booth, where Isaiah and Elijah were working. "God used them to save my life. I was just a kid. We're all just kids." She laughed. "It's a good thing how much God loves his kids."

Large Print Books
by Robin Merrill

New Beginnings
Knocking
Kicking
Searching
Knitting
Working
Splitting

Piercehaven Trilogy
Piercehaven
Windmills
Trespass

Shelter Trilogy
Shelter
Daniel
Revival

Wing and a Prayer Mysteries
The Whistle Blower
The Showstopper
The Pinch Runner
The Prima Donna

Made in the USA
Las Vegas, NV
16 January 2023